# PRAISE FOR LAURA BEST

## *A Sure Cure for Witchcraft*

"In *A Sure Cure for Witchcraft*, author Laura Best takes readers on a beautifully written and thrilling adventure about friendship that alternates between the past and the present. Middle-grade readers will gobble up this page-turner, which focuses on the challenges faced by seventeenth-century Lilli—including accusations of witchcraft and being forced to move to the new world—and present-day Lilly, who's racing against the clock to unravel the mysterious connection between herself and a neighbour. Thought-provoking and inspiring, this book is sure to spark many conversations about women's empowerment!"

**–Wendy McLeod MacKnight, author of *The CopyCat, The Frame-Up, and It's a Mystery, Pig Face!***

"A mystery, some witchery, and a touch of the supernatural make for a compelling read about the power of friendship. A beautifully written and evocative tale."

**–Julie Lawson, author of *A Blinding Light***

## *The Family Way*

"This prequel to Laura Best's two previous novels about Cammie is another magnificent example of middle-grade historical fiction that truly resonates with readers of all ages....

The author brilliantly captures the small-town setting and provides an insightful glimpse into the heartbreaking true story of the Ideal Maternity Home and its terrible secret."

**–Canadian Children's Book News**

"Tulia is a wonderful main charac--- -- intriguing combination of adult and child....By the end of the nitely more aware of the circums makes the history come alive."

**–Canadian Review of Materials, *h***

D111173E

# ALSO BY LAURA BEST

# A Sure Cure
## *for*
# WITCHCRAFT

### Laura Best

NIMBUS
PUBLISHING LTD.

Nimbus Publishing Limited
3660 Strawberry Hill Street, Halifax, NS, B3K 5A9
(902) 455-4286 nimbus.ca

Printed and bound in Canada
Cover Design: Heather Bryan
Editor: Penelope Jackson
Editor for the press: Whitney Moran
NB1530

*This story is a work of fiction. Names, characters, incidents, and places, including organizations and institutions, are used fictitiously.*

Library and Archives Canada Cataloguing in Publication

Title: A sure cure for witchcraft / Laura Best.
Names: Best, Laura (Laura A.), author.
Identifiers: Canadiana (print) 20210214430 | Canadiana (ebook) 20210214481 | ISBN 9781771089777 (softcover) | ISBN 9781771089845 (EPUB)
Classification: LCC PS8603.E777 S87 2021 | DDC C813/.6—dc23

Nimbus Publishing acknowledges the financial support for its publishing activities from the Government of Canada, the Canada Council for the Arts, and from the Province of Nova Scotia. We are pleased to work in partnership with the Province of Nova Scotia to develop and promote our creative industries for the benefit of all Nova Scotians.

*For my German ancestors who braved the harsh Atlantic to follow their dreams.*

*Even in a world that is being shipwrecked, remain brave and strong.*

—HILDEGARD VON BINGEN

# PROLOGUE

L ILLY FOUND THE FIRST MEMORY WHEN SHE WAS FIVE, hidden between the covers of a book with blank pages she received for her birthday. When she pulled a green wax crayon from the box and touched it to the empty page, she suddenly remembered another book she used to have. When she mentioned this to her parents, her father quickly spoke up.

"There was no other book," he said.

"Yes, there was," insisted Lilly. "Don't you remember? It had brown covers. There were pictures and words. I used to read from it."

Her father laughed. "You can't read a word. You haven't even been to school."

"You must be remembering a dream," said her mother. An odd expression settled on her lips. "Now, sit up and draw me a pretty picture with your crayon."

The first picture Lilly drew was of a large leaf. She added veins and a stem. Next, she drew a flower with pretty blue petals. "That's a cornflower. It's for making medicine."

"Making medicine?" Her mother sounded amused. "How could you possibly know that? You have never even seen a cornflower."

"I remember it from before. A woman gave me one, for a gift. But it was when I lived *There*, not *Here*," said Lilly, and she continued to draw. Yellow, orange, red, violet, and blue—Lilly filled the page with colour. Of all the gifts she received on her birthday, the book with the empty pages was her favourite. Somehow it awoke wonderful memories inside her. She carried the book around for the entire day, never letting it out of her sight.

"You should put the book on your dresser," her mother said when nighttime came, but Lilly insisted on keeping it with her. Her mother looked at the bound pages clutched so tightly in Lilly's hands and smiled. But Lilly did not smile. Her mother and father were wrong. There had been another book with drawings and words. She'd opened the covers. She'd turned the pages. She'd read the words. It was a long time ago, before she ever came to New Germany.

It wasn't a dream.

In the memory she was also called Lilly. Her hair was thin and wispy and long and the colour of yellow straw, tied up in braids. She was standing on a wide riverbank; rippling water moved across her reflection. When she waved, the reflection in the water waved back at her, but it wasn't the same face she saw in the mirror when she brushed her teeth every night. The face in the water was hers, but it belonged to someone else too, someone she had never seen before, someone much older.

Another memory came with laughter, rich and full. The sound reminded her of the babbling brook where she and her father went to catch fish. She couldn't remember if she was the one laughing or if it was someone else. At night she danced and pulled roots from the earth, and smiled into the moon's soft, round face. She sang sweet songs with the birds. She was happy.

Some nights Lilly dreamt about the drawings in the leather-bound book, and the words on the pages that made no sense to her. A hand flipped through those pages, through the veins and stems, leaves and blossoms. The pictures swayed and bowed and quivered upon the page. The drawings were fine, detailed, and perfect. The book meant something precious and lasting. She'd held it many times, turned the pages with great care. It felt familiar and right. It was one of her favourite memories. There was also a mysterious cinnamon-haired woman who made her laugh. After a night of dreams, Lilly would open the book she got for her birthday and draw more plants on the empty pages.

"I know you," said Lilly the day a strange woman came to visit. She was sitting at the kitchen table sipping tea with Lilly's mother. Her hair was long and thick, the colour of cinnamon, and her eyes were emerald green. She was the cinnamon-haired woman from Lilly's dreams.

"Lilly, this is our neighbour, Alice Goodwin. She moved into the Jennings house a while back. I'm afraid you've never met her," said her mother. "Alice is a herbalist and she knows all about plants and herbs. She's going to open a practise right here in New Germany. She is the one who sent you the book on your birthday."

Lilly ran off to find the book and brought it back to show Alice.

"Look at all the lovely drawings," said Alice, studying the pictures with great interest. "When I heard that a little girl down the road was having a birthday, I wanted to send something. Everyone loves gifts on their birthday." Her parents had tied bright balloons onto the mailbox that day with a big sign that said *Happy Birthday Lilly*. "I can see you are putting the gift to good use."

"Lilly is quite the artist *and* storyteller," said her mother, smiling. "She's been inventing plants and making up stories to go with them."

Lilly scowled. The plants were real. She'd told her mother many times—and so were the stories.

"I see you have drawn some chamomile, and that looks like feverfew!" said Alice, pointing to the page.

"Feverfew?" Lilly's mother pulled the book from Alice's hands and gave a small laugh. "Lilly doesn't know what feverfew is…is that even a word?"

"Absolutely," said Alice. "It's used for treating fever and headaches, and all sorts of ailments. It's an important healing plant that's been used for centuries."

"I don't know anything about healing plants," said Lilly's mother as she set the book on top of the refrigerator, "and neither does Lilly." She forced a smile.

"You had a different name," said Lilly as she reached for a cookie on the plate.

"What do you mean a different name?" said Alice. She smiled and then sipped her tea.

"When I knew you from before."

"How interesting," said Alice, playing along with Lilly's unusual talk. "I've always imagined being someone else. Do you remember what my name used to be?"

When Lilly shook her head, her mother's face turned red and she laughed. "But I remember you talked to the plants," continued Lilly.

"But did the plants talk back? That's the important question," said Alice in a playful voice. Lilly wanted to laugh. "I do like growing things, and talking to plants sounds like fun. Perhaps one day you can help out in my garden. We can carry on a conversation with the dahlias. Who knows, maybe they'll answer us back."

"Plants can't talk," giggled Lilly.

"'You talked to the plants,'" said Lilly's mother, shaking her head. "How does she make these things up?"

Reaching for another cookie, Lilly took a bite and added, "And you made people better."

"That is enough, Lilly," said her mother, firmly. She was no longer smiling. "I'm afraid you've never met Alice before. I already told you, this is the first time she's been to the house." As her mother reached for the teapot, Alice Goodwin smiled at Lilly. It was the smile of someone who knows a secret that they are not about to tell.

"Our Lilly has a wild imagination," said her mother, turning back toward Alice with the teapot in her hand.

"Einstein did say that imagination is more important than knowledge," said Alice, continuing to smile at Lilly.

"Now run along," said her mother, pouring more tea in Alice's cup. It was then Lilly noticed the unusual pendant Alice was wearing.

"Do you like it?" said Alice when she saw Lilly staring. Lilly quickly nodded.

"It's very pretty. What kind of stone is it?" asked Lilly's mother.

"It's called a labradorite stone, but," said Alice, her eyes lighting up as she spoke, "a much better name for labradorite is rainbow moonstone. This necklace has been in my family for centuries, and do you know what, Lilly?" Lilly shook her head, anxious to hear more. "There's a wonderfully delicious story that goes along with it, a story that holds a mysterious secret. But," said Alice sitting back in her chair, "it's a family secret, and I can't tell." Lilly begged to hear the story behind the rainbow moonstone, until finally Alice gave in.

"Very well then, but you must promise to never ever repeat the story I am about to tell," said Alice seriously. Lilly promised; with all her heart, she promised. More than anything, she needed to know what the mysterious secret was. She moved in closer and Alice began.

"This is the story that was told to me when I was about your age. The stone was a gift given to one of my ancestors back in the eighteenth century by a dear friend. These friends spent many days together exploring the forest near where they lived. But the day came when they had to part ways, as one was setting out on an adventure to the New World. That is what they called Nova Scotia back then. It was not known if her friend ever made it to her destination, for many people at that time did not survive the trip across the ocean."

*Didn't survive?* Lilly's eyes grew wide with apprehension.

"It was a torturous trip, from what I've read. Many people on these ships became sick and died. The water was horrible and so was the food. The ships were dark and smelly. There weren't even any bathrooms."

"No bathrooms?" Lilly couldn't imagine a trip being so horrible.

"That is true," said Alice as she continued. "Now, the friend who was leaving didn't want to say goodbye, but before she left, she gave her friend this lovely pendant." Alice reached for the labradorite stone, squeezing it between her fingers. "The story goes that when the time is right, the pendant will somehow unite these two friends again."

"That's quite a story," said Lilly's mother.

"Is it true?" Lilly seemed unable to take her eyes off the stone now that she knew its mysterious secret.

"It's true if you believe it's true," said Alice. "Anything is true if you believe."

# CHAPTER ONE

**T**HE DAY AFTER LILLI'S FIFTH BIRTHDAY, A BREEZE, QUITE warm for September, rustled the leaves on the sycamore trees, causing them to sway and bow in a most peculiar manner. The circular motion of the trees caught Mutter's attention. She looked down at Lilli playing with some pink and brown pebbles in the dooryard. When a white dove landed on a post near the place where Lilli was playing and cooed three times before flying off, Mutter knew the time had come. She did not imagine that Vater would be at all pleased.

"Stand up straight and remember to smile," said Mutter moments before she knocked at Alisz's door. Lilli was mesmerized by the flowers growing nearby: bright hues of violet, yellow, orange, sapphire, and pink. Never before had she seen such lovely colours, certainly not in their own dooryard. Mutter and Vater grew things to eat and fields of flax, not plants with beauty and colour.

Friedrich reached out and grabbed a handful of his sister's hair. Mutter quickly pulled him back. "Pay attention," she said, quickly smoothing Lilli's hair into place and touching the tip of her nose.

"Who is this woman?" Lilli asked, seeking Mutter's reassurance once more before the door opened.

"I have told you already. Alisz is family. A distant cousin on my mother's side. Now smile." Mutter stood straight and tall, clearing her throat as they waited to be welcomed inside the small cottage. But the moment the door opened and Alisz's voice rang out, Lilli's smile disappeared.

"Marta, my dear! Come in, come in," Alisz chorused, her voice lashing out like a whip. "I thought perhaps you might come today," she said, her face beaming with delight. Lilli knew that was impossible. Mutter had only made up her mind to come that very morning.

"It is about time I brought Lilli," said Mutter, her one arm wrapped around Friedrich, the other now encompassing Alisz in an embrace. "As you know, Lilli has just turned five, and five years is a very long time. I did not want you to think that we had gone back on our word to you."

"I have always had faith you would keep your word, Marta. Believe it or not, I have been counting the days. Please, do come in."

Lilli felt her legs turn to wood. Suddenly this did not feel like such a good idea. Even Vater had put up a fuss moments before they were about to leave. But Mutter had looked at him and quietly said, "I will not go back on my word."

"For goodness' sake, go inside. Alisz will not harm you." Mutter pushed on the back of Lilli's head, sending her stumbling through the doorway.

"Now, Marta, do not blame the poor child for being frightened. It is not every day that you meet a witch—is it, Lilli?" Alisz tossed her cinnamon-coloured hair as she spoke, her eyes sparkled with mischief.

Lilli's mouth dropped wide open. She had never met anyone like Alisz before. Mutter sometimes visited with Frau Weber, who often scolded Lilli for not sitting still. Frau Weber would never laugh and call herself a witch, and yet here was this woman, someone she had never met before, doing just that. Vater had warned Lilli about witches in the past. "There were those who came before us, Lilli, good Christian people, left to wither and die at the hand of witches," he would say. They can even slide down the chimney in the middle of the night and bewitch you while you sleep. Vater had stories, so many of them, about people who had been bewitched. Sometimes the stories frightened Lilli and she would run to Mutter, crying.

"There, there," Mutter would say. "You must not listen to what Vater tells you. There is no such thing as a witch. No one is capable of performing the things he has described. It is only his belief because of the things he was told when he was young, but you must remember that not all beliefs are true. This is one that is not. Vater means well, but he is frightened by the things he does not understand."

Lilli quickly looked back toward Mutter, trying to sort out her confusion about this strange woman now standing before them, but Mutter did not look at all confused. She was beaming a bright smile that quickly burst into laughter. There was something pleasing about the vibration that rose then from Mutter's throat. Lilli had never seen Mutter's eyes dance with such glee before. This Alisz made Mutter very happy.

"You must stop teasing Lilli. You will have her believing in witches too, and we simply cannot have that," said Mutter.

Alisz's house smelled strange inside. Spice and perfume—it was a mixture of both wrapped into one. Yet, there was something more, some strange fragrance, something that Lilli could not name.

"Let me take a good look at you," said Alisz, gazing down at Lilli as if she were a prized goose in the butcher's shop. She touched a lock of Lilli's hair. "It is fine—like a baby's. The colour of flax," she said, "and your eyes are as blue as an indigo sky. You are a very pretty girl." Something hot pinched Lilli's cheeks. She pulled at Mutter and hid her face in the fabric of her dress. No one had ever told Lilli she was pretty before.

"Alisz is not going to bite you. Do not be so silly," said Mutter, untwining her garb from Lilli's fingers.

"You just never know, Lilli. I might bite." Lilli's eyes grew wide once again. "But only if you were to bite me first. You would not do that, would you?" Alisz's musical laugh startled Friedrich, and he let out a sharp cry. Mutter made a few shushing noises, and he soon quieted.

"So tell me, Lilli Eickle, what have you done in the five years since I last saw you? I hope you have been keeping a record of sorts."

"Alisz was there the night you were born," explained Mutter quietly.

Lilli had been told the story of her birth many times, about the beautiful midwife who held her up to the night sky right after she was born.

"The breeze carried the sweet scent of lily-of-the-valley," Mutter would say.

"Is that how I got my name?" Lilli would ask each time.

"And a more fitting name has never been found. I knew it to be true the moment Alisz spoke your name into the night. And then a moonbeam touched you on the forehead, declaring that good fortune would follow you always," Mutter would say.

"I most certainly was there when you were born," said Alisz now, smiling down at Lilli. "And if I must say, you were the sweetest babe I had ever laid eyes on. Of course you had more important things on your mind than being admired for your beauty. You came out hungry as a bear and you made sure everyone knew it."

Alisz's words rained down like a thousand silky feathers tickling her all at once. Lilli could not stop a giggle from slipping out.

"Come, I have made tea," said Alisz, motioning for Mutter to sit at the table. Setting Friedrich on the floor, Mutter told Lilli to keep watch over him. As the women quickly engaged in conversation, Lilli became spellbound by the words and laughter filling the corners and crevices of Alisz's small house. Strange that Mutter had not taken her to visit with Alisz before now.

When the tea grew cold and the words finally slowed, Mutter picked Friedrich up off the floor. "It is time to go," she said. "Alisz would like for you to stay, Lilli. So that you may get acquainted."

"Acquainted?" Lilli said in a small voice. She had only met Alisz a short while ago, and now Mutter wanted her to stay. Alisz looked down at Lilli. Her smile formed a warm place in Lilli's heart.

"Would you stay and keep me company today, Lilli? We can walk in the garden and talk to the plants. I have so much planned."

"Talk to the plants?" laughed Lilli, suddenly forgetting her shyness.

"Why certainly, plants like to be talked to as well as you and I. Lonely plants do not grow very well." Another ripple of laughter filled Lilli's throat. No one she knew talked to plants. It sounded silly.

"So, what do you say, Lilli Eickle, will you visit with me for the day?"

Lilli looked toward Mutter with uncertainty.

"Vater does not approve of my friendship with Alisz, but it is too late for him to complain now," Mutter had said as they walked toward Alisz's cottage that morning. "I told Vater it is high time you met Alisz. It is important that you get to know her."

When Lilli asked why it was important, Mutter did not answer.

"Do not look so worried, Lilli. Alisz will take good care of you," said Mutter as she waved goodbye. "You will be safe with her. We will be back before you know it."

# CHAPTER TWO

**L**ILLI WATCHED MUTTER DISAPPEAR FROM SIGHT AS THE papery wings of a moth fluttered inside her. "Come see what I have to show you," Alisz said as she reached out to take Lilli's hand. Lilli turned back toward Alisz. Her throat began to ache. Would Mutter really come back for her? How long would she be gone? Alisz's smile did little to reassure her that all was well. She blinked away the tears from her eyes, hoping that Mutter would not stay away too long.

A small gathering of song sparrows was perched in the trees outside Alisz's home, releasing a sweet melody into the gentle breeze. Leaves whispered, blades of grass softly murmured when Lilli and Alisz walked past. Reaching the garden behind the house, Alisz searched through the foliage, moving the leaves and flower stems all about. She called out in a curious manner, "Mandrake, where are you, dear mandrake? I saw you just a few days ago. I want to introduce you to my friend, Lilli. She has come to spend the day with us. You must not be shy or she will not visit us again." Alisz's voice blended in with the song sparrow's melody. Spreading the leafy foliage apart, she revealed a plant hidden closer to the earth. Her voice leapt with excitement.

"Why, there you are, you little rascal! I knew you could not hide from me for long! Come Lilli, and see this shy devil." Lilli stepped closer. "Do you think she should be punished for hiding on us?" Lilli looked at Alisz and quickly shook her head.

"People used to think the mandrake roots resembled a human body and it would even shriek when pulled from the ground, and if someone heard its cry they would die."

"Plants cannot shriek!" Lilli laughed. What a preposterous notion. They giggled until it no longer seemed funny, and then the lines in Alisz's face grew serious.

"You will hear many strange things in life, but remember this, Lilli Eickle—lies are borne out of ignorance and fear. Nothing more."

Lilli had never met anyone like Alisz before, with the ability to make the most ordinary thing, like a plant, sound so interesting. And never before had she heard a voice filled with such spiciness. Together they explored all there was to see, from the tallest plant to the smallest bit of greenery. They chased after bugs, sang with the birds, and whispered secrets to the wind. As they walked about the garden searching for plants, Lilli soon forgot about Mutter and Friedrich.

There were so many wonderful things to see. Alisz said that every plant had a special name, a special purpose. "One day you will know all there is to know about plants, dear Lilli. But today we will simply enjoy their beauty." With so many plants in the garden, Lilli wondered how that would be possible. How would she ever know everything about them?

The sun arced across the sky as the day dwindled away. When it began to touch the treeline, Alisz said it would soon be time for her to go. Lilli was not sure she wanted Mutter and Friedrich to come back for her just yet. She wanted to stay with Alisz a while longer.

"Now, before you go on your way, you may choose a flower to take with you. It will be my gift to you," said Alisz.

"I like these," said Lilli, racing toward the outer edge of the garden, where some tall plants were growing. She reached out to one of the bright blue flowers, touching its delicate petals. Would Alisz really let her take some of them home?

"You have chosen wisely. That is a cornflower, a symbol of hope, and one of my favourites, although I must admit I have many, many favourites. So many that perhaps they are all my favourite. But that is impossible. Every flower cannot be your favourite. Can it?"

Lilli shook her head. She couldn't help but giggle. Alisz's silly talk made her heart sing. Why had Mutter not taken her to meet Alisz before now? "Hurry," said Lilli, anxiously waiting beside the cornflowers for Alisz. Bees were buzzing as they moved among the flowers. Alisz seemed to be taking her time. Mutter and Friedrich would soon be here.

"I want to take a big handful home to Mutter," said Lilli when Alisz finally reached her. There were so many of the pretty blue flowers in the garden, surely Alisz would not mind. It would make Mutter happy. Sometimes they picked wildflowers for on the table.

"No, Lilli," said Alisz, "that is not the way it is done. One flower—you may have but one. Flowers are a gift from nature. If we take too many, there will be none left for others to enjoy."

Mutter would say she should be grateful for one, but one flower did not seem like enough when there were so many in the garden. Seeing Lilli's disappointment, Alisz added, "It is our duty to honour nature. One day you will understand." Lilli was not sure that was true. She did not know what it meant to honour nature.

A large bumblebee landed on a flower in front of them and immediately began collecting nectar and pollen. "Hello, dear bumblebee," said Alisz, reaching out to the buzzing creature. "What message do you have for us today?"

"It will sting!" said Lilli, jumping back. Mutter had warned her not to anger a bee, to keep her distance.

"Shhh," said Alisz, holding a finger to her lips. "We must listen carefully to what the bee has to say, for bees are filled with a wisdom all of their own." She held one hand to her ear and bent down toward the buzzing insect. Lilli watched in silent fascination as the bee hovered close to Alisz.

"I see...that is quite interesting," she said as if the bee were actually speaking to her. "I will pass your message along to my friend Lilli. Now, away you go." Flying to a nearby cornflower, the bee disappeared momentarily from sight before flying away, its legs swollen with bright yellow pollen.

"What did it say?" Lilli was desperate to know.

"Our messenger today was reminding me to ask for the flower's permission before we pick it." Alisz bent down close to one of the cornflowers. Lilli waited to see what she would do next.

Alisz closed her eyes. "May I have permission, lovely cornflower, to pick your beautiful bloom for my friend Lilli?" Several seconds passed before Alisz opened her eyes. She breathed in the flower's delicate fragrance before carefully plucking it from the stem. "Thank you for your sacrifice, dear cornflower," she said, giving it to Lilli.

"But flowers do not know," said Lilli as she waited for the sound of Alisz's musical laughter to fill the air. This was just more of Alisz's silly talk.

"Flowers most certainly do know!" said Alisz, sounding surprised by Lilli's statement. "That is why we ask for permission whenever we take something from Mother Earth. And always remember to say thank you. Do you understand? Ask first, and then give thanks." Lilli could see how important this was. She nodded her head, and Alisz smiled. Lilli held the flower gently between her fingers. She would remember.

When the sun dropped down into the trees, Mutter returned,

carrying Friedrich in her arms. "I hope you behaved yourself," she said as they walked the path homeward. Lilli held the cornflower proudly in her hand—her gift from Alisz. When they reached home, Lilli put the flower in a jar of water and set it on the table. She presented it to Vater that evening when he came in from working in the field.

"What is this you have?" he said, taking the jar from Lilli. Smelling the flower, he smiled and said, "Only one?"

"It is a cornflower and it is important only to take one," said Lilli, repeating what Alisz had taught her that day.

"I see," said Vater as he continued to admire the indigo bloom. "And what else do you know about this cornflower?" He set the jar in the middle of the table.

"That you must ask permission before you pick it," she said, climbing onto Vater's lap. Mutter hesitated while setting the table for the evening meal.

"Permission? Who do you ask permission from?" said Vater. He looked up at Mutter, smiling. Lilli could see he did not understand.

"Why, the flower," said Lilli. "And after you pick it you must say thank you."

"Who told you this—Mutter?" said Vater, still sounding amused by Lilli's whimsical talk.

"It was the bee."

"The bee? You were talking to a bee?"

Lilli sighed. Why could Vater not understand? "No, Vater. The bee told Alisz and then *she* told me what it said."

Cutlery rattled. "Come, Lilli," Mutter said. "Help me set the table."

Anger flashed across Vater's face. He jumped to his feet, facing Mutter.

"Tell me, Marta, this is not so."

Mutter laid a hand on Lilli's head and gently smiled. She pulled back her shoulders and looked directly at Vater. There was resolve in her voice as she quietly said, "You knew this day would come, Karl. You have always known this day would come."

# CHAPTER THREE

STREAKS OF LIGHT STREAMED THROUGH THE CANOPY of trees as Lilli and Alisz followed a narrow footpath, wet with late morning dew. Lilli looked up in time to see a hawk soaring in the cloudless sky.

"Look, Alisz!" she said, pointing upward at the majestic bird now screeching down at them. It circled gracefully, gliding with its wings spread wide open.

"The hawk is a sign meant for you, Lilli—from the Goddess," said Alisz, sounding pleased.

"A sign for me?" Lilli didn't like the sound of that. Vater said that hawks would sometimes steal chickens from the dooryard. How could a hawk be a good sign?

"Oma used to say a hawk was a symbol of freedom and flight— the freedom to answer the call that stirs deep inside your heart. Healing is your calling, Lilli. The hawk is a sign. Now come, we must continue on our quest. We still have far to go."

Birds flittered along the path, releasing their songs into the wind. Lilli became distracted by the sights along the way. Two squirrels ran down a tree not far from Lilli, racing across the ground near her feet. She pulled her basket close, afraid they might jump after the small round loaf of unleavened bread inside. The bread was a gift for Mother Elder, the tree spirit that lived inside the elder tree. They dare not pick the elderflowers without leaving something in return.

"Our elders are teachers and wisdom keepers and we must always honour them," Alisz had said before they left the cottage that morning. "The same is true for the elder tree."

"Why are we taking bread?" Were they to stop for a lunch along the way?

"The bread is for Mother Elder, the goddess of all the elders, and we do not wish to anger her in any way. It is why we take an offering and ask permission to harvest her bounty."

Lilli knew about respecting the elders. Frau Schubert, an elder from the village, would sit outside her home and call out a greeting to the people passing by. Many people would mumble a quick greeting in return but continue on. She was near blind; her face and hands were weathered and old. One day she called out to Lilli and Mutter, and Mutter slowed her steps. Lilli had begged her not to stop.

"Do not be afraid," Mutter had said. "Frau Schubert is lonely and in need of company. The least we can do is listen."

It did not take long before Frau Schubert was telling them a story of a village long ago that had become overrun with rats. The mention of the furry rodents made Lilli gasp, but that did not stop Frau Schubert from continuing. She told them how the villagers promised to pay a stranger to lure the rats away.

"He had a pipe with magical powers and called himself the Pied Piper." Frau Schubert leaned in closer to Lilli. Her eyes lit up and her face filled with expression. "Thousands of rats scurried out into the street that day and followed the piper when he played," said Frau Schubert, stretching her arms out wide. But the story did not end there. After the piper had rid the village of all the rats, the villagers refused to pay him for his work. To get back at the villagers for cheating him, he used his magical pipe to lead all the children out of the village, the same way he had the rats.

"Beware those who do not keep their promises," came Frau Schubert's stern warning when she reached the end of her story. She pointed a gnarled finger at Lilli and smiled.

"Why did Frau Schubert tell us a story about rats?" said Lilli as she and Mutter continued on their travels. Rats were horrible creatures, even rats that followed a piper and ended up drowned in a river.

"You must remember, Lilli, that with age comes wisdom," Mutter had said. "The story was not about rats, but about the importance of keeping one's word." Lilli vowed then that she would always keep her promises.

Still preoccupied by the squirrels, Lilli suddenly realized that Alisz was nowhere in sight. What if she became lost? She called out, her heart thumping like the quick beating of partridge wings.

"I am here," Alisz answered through the trees.

"Wait for me!" cried Lilli. She hurried toward the sound of Alisz's voice, frantically pushing aside bushes in her way. She hoped she would not be scolded for lagging behind. But when she caught up, Alisz smiled and said, "Did you see anything interesting in your travels?"

"Two squirrels chasing each other through the trees. I thought they might steal the bread," said Lilli, catching her breath.

"And is the loaf safe?"

"I kept the basket close," said Lilli. She lifted the cloth to show Alisz.

Alisz nodded. "Very good," she said. "Today, you are the guardian of the bread. You have done your job well and learned a valuable lesson in the process."

Lilli's face became warm. She should not have allowed herself to become distracted.

"Now come," said Alisz. "Mother Elder awaits."

Determined not to be left behind once again, she stayed close to Alisz's side.

"Will Mother Elder tell us stories?" Lilli asked as they made their way through the trees, but Alisz did not answer. Lilli was anxious to learn more about this elder wisdom Alisz spoke of. She didn't think that Frau Schubert was nearly as wise as the elder tree, but Mutter had said there was wisdom in the stories she told and they should pay attention when she spoke.

Their quest to find Mother Elder led them past saplings and evergreens as they continued their journey through the dense forest growth. Many trees looked old to Lilli. Surely one of them was the wise elder they sought, but Alisz walked on.

"We will soon be there," said Alisz when Lilli finally asked how much farther they had to go. She stopped when they came to a small clearing in the forest where the sun had room to frolic and dance.

"We are here," Alisz said at last. In the distance was a large tree, its boughs heavy with creamy white flowers. They walked slowly, approaching the tree with reverence and respect. Alisz motioned for Lilli to step forward with the small round loaf. When the offering was in place at the base of the tree, Alisz closed her eyes and opened her arms wide.

"Mother Elder, we come respectfully asking permission to pick your beautiful flowers. If it pleases you, we will use your flowers to make a healing tea to cure others of their ailments." The elder leaves rustled as Lilli waited for Mother Elder to speak, but she could not hear anything coming from the wise tree-spirit. Moments passed. Alisz bowed her head slightly and whispered a quiet thank you, satisfied that Mother Elder had granted them permission.

"The elder bark has valleys and hills," said Alisz, touching the sacred tree. Lilli laid a hand on the wrinkled tree trunk; she was sure she could feel this elder wisdom Alisz spoke of. She removed the harvesting bag from her basket and gave it to Alisz.

"We must be careful not to bruise the blossoms," said Alisz as she pulled the white clusters from the stems. She gently shook the elderflowers before placing them inside the bag. "And we certainly do not want to drink tea that has bugs in it." Lilli curled up her nose. Smiling, Alisz invited Lilli to help. As Alisz explained the many medicinal purposes for the floras, Lilli paid close attention, carefully sealing Alisz's words in her memory. Little by little, she would learn the language and wisdom of plants and trees.

"This I find very interesting," said Alisz as they walked homeward, their harvesting bags now full. "It is said that women would often kiss the elder to ensure their babies would have good fortune, and another story tells that it is unlucky to chop down the elder and make a cradle, for the spirit living inside the tree will pinch the child black and blue and the child will not sleep."

"Is there really a spirit living inside the tree?" asked Lilli. She had learned not to laugh about the unusual stories Alisz told.

Alisz thought for a moment. "We all have different beliefs, Lilli, and if those beliefs do not hurt others, then where is the harm? Besides, it is fun to hear these stories. Tell me, dear Lilli, do you want to believe?"

"Yes," Lilli said quickly.

"Then you have answered your own question. Now, let us get these elderflowers back to the stillroom. There is more work to do."

Back at the stillroom, they spread the blossoms out on the worktable to dry. "We have had a most productive day," said Alisz as she looked at the blossoms spread before them. "We will return when the elderberries are ripe and we will make a winter remedy."

"Winter remedy is for coughs," said Lilli, remembering Alisz's teachings.

"Indeed it is. You are a most eager student, my young apprentice," said Alisz, laughing.

As the sun arced across the afternoon sky and began its slow descent below the treetops, Alisz brought out a brown leather-bound book. The cover appeared aged, the pages slightly turned and yellowed with time. "Come sit with me," she said to Lilli. "It is time I shared this with you. I have been waiting for a sign, and that sign came today. There is much to be learned, and it will take years."

"How many years?" Lilli looked up into Alisz's smiling face. The book was thick. Lilli was entering her eighth summer. How many more summers would it take before she knew everything in the book? It was a question Alisz did not have the answer to.

Settling onto a bench in her garden, Alisz carefully opened the book.

"What are those?" Lilli asked, pointing to the tiny symbols on the page.

"They are words."

"What are words?" Lilli looked up at Alisz, perplexed. She had never heard of words. What were they used for?

Alisz smiled. "Words convey ideas. They are knowledge and wisdom, and will one day bring about the end to all the ignorance and fear in the world. This book belonged to my oma," Alisz said, slowly turning the pages. There were drawings of plants on some pages, while other pages were filled with the symbols Alisz called words.

"She was accused of being a witch. Mutter and I were there when they took her away. I was about your age. I told Mutter we needed to help her. 'There is no help for someone accused of witch-craft,' she said. 'They will only take us away, too.' We were helpless to do anything."

Alisz paused as a long shadow passed over her face. She stared off into the distance. Clearing her throat, she looked down at Lilli and forced a smile.

"But that was a long time ago. We cannot live with one foot

stuck in the past. Life is to be lived in the here and now."

"*Was* she a witch?" asked Lilli, suddenly curious to know. Vater often spoke about witches and their evil ways. He worried that a witch might one day cast a spell on their family.

"Not a witch, dear Lilli. She was a healer. Just like you and me."

"Like me?" Surely Alisz was mistaken. She was only seven. She did not know anything about healing.

"Yes, Lilli, like you. I saw it the night you were born. There are people in this world—chosen ones. They are born with a gift to heal others. You have that gift inside you. As I said earlier, the hawk today was a sign from the Goddess."

Lilli looked down at the book filled with words and drawings. "Someday, I will learn to read all the words in the world and I will make a book just like this one," she said as Alisz closed the covers.

"Who knows, dear, sweet Lilli," said Alisz, smiling, "perhaps one day *this* book will be yours."

# CHAPTER FOUR

"**D**ID I TELL EVER YOU THAT A CROWN MADE OF GUNDER-mann is supposed to be a cure for witchcraft?" said Alisz, carefully examining the plant Lilli was holding before her. Alisz liked to sketch in nature, with the sun and wind sending their blessing. Usually Lilli enjoyed watching her work, but today was different. Somewhere through the thick growth of trees, a babbling brook was calling out to her.

"Not another foolish superstition," said Lilli. Over the years, Alisz had told her about dozens of plants capable of curing witchcraft. Some sounded so silly that Lilli couldn't help laughing. There was no such thing as witches. Everyone should know that. She knew that from the first day she met Alisz.

"And a sure cure at that," added Alisz. "But such ignorance will not discourage me from adding gundermann to the book. Despite all that, it has many wonderful uses, none of which is to ward off evil. However, I will make a note of that, for interest's sake if nothing else.

Someday, someone might want to know how foolish people once were. Now, this next bit of information should cheer you—gundermann is also known as catsfoot."

"Catsfoot is a fun name," laughed Lilli.

"Miau! I thought you would like that," said Alisz, smiling as she playfully clawed the air like a cat. "Now hold it steady, wiggly worm." Alisz kneeled in closer to study the small round leaves and purple flowers quivering between Lilli's pinched fingers.

"It is not me," said Lilli, chasing after a stray lock of hair that was dancing across her face. "There is too much wind today." The breeze continued to shift the herb she was holding out for Alisz to examine.

"The keeper of the winds is playing games with you," laughed Alisz. "Come closer. You are way too high. You are sprouting up like a fireweed these days." It was true. Not long ago, Mutter had lengthened Lilli's tunic again.

"You hold it," said Lilli, pushing the plant toward Alisz.

"I cannot draw and hold it at the same time, silly."

Lilli looked over her shoulder. "The brook makes wonderful music," she said. The sound was like laughter. She was anxious to discover which direction it flowed and if there were any creatures living along its banks. Alisz said it would be a day of discovery. The Goddess had come to her in a dream and told her so. But so far Lilli had not discovered a thing.

"I am still looking," said Alisz. "I need to understand how the leaves and flowers grow in relation to one another. The flowers are so delicate. The sketch needs to be exact, otherwise whoever owns this book in the future will not be able to recognize gundermann from chamomile. You are just too curious to stand still. That is all."

"The book will *always* belong to you," said Lilli. Alisz often studied the pages in her book for hours when looking for a remedy. There were so many words, so many recipes and sketches. Even Alisz, with all of her wisdom and knowledge, would not be able to remember it all without help from the book.

"Life is filled with mystery, my dear Lilli. There is much for you to see, much to experience. We never know what will come our way, how circumstances could quickly put us on a different path. But we must stay open to all possibilities," said Alisz.

Settling back onto the grass, Alisz reached for the book and turned to an empty page. Carefully dipping the quill into the ink, she touched it to the thin parchment. With a steady hand, she began making fine strokes on the page. The tip glided across the parchment. Lilli never grew tired of watching Alisz sketch. She never made mistakes. Her drawings were flawless, each curve of a leaf, every stem and vein and flowerhead shaped perfectly. She would study a plant for a long time before drawing it in her book.

Alisz looked up at Lilli and gently fanned the page, waiting for the ink to dry. "Go, inquisitive little worm. Explore to your heart's content," she said. Pulling the gundermann from Lilli's fingers, she quickly ate it. Alisz never wasted the gifts the Earth Goddess provided.

"Are you sure?" said Lilli. She did not want to appear too anxious.

"I want to transcribe these things onto the page beneath my drawing, and then I will join you. Run along, but do not go far."

Somewhere through the hardwood trees, the burbling brook called out to Lilli. She hurried through the undergrowth to explore. Stopping beside the water's edge, she wondered what creatures lived beneath the surface. She followed the brook down to where it grew wider. Two rocks jutting out of the water would put her closer to where the water was deepest. Perhaps she could play with her reflection if she were farther away from the shaded shoreline. Pulling her dress up to her knees, she hopped out onto the rocks. Her reflection was waiting for her in the slow current, and she waved. The water gurgled and flowed. Lilli became caught up in its musical song.

"Lilli! Come away from there. You are too close!" Lilli turned at the sound of Alisz's voice, and her foot slipped from the mossy rock.

Her arms flailed outward as she struggled to keep from falling. Alisz let out a scream and raced toward the brook just as Lilli plunged into the water. She was breathing heavily when she reached Lilli, who was now climbing out onto dry land. Grabbing fast to Lilli, she pulled her close.

"You had me near frightened to death," she said, her chest heaving.

"I am fine, Alisz. Truly. The water was not deep." Lilli looked up into Alisz's terrified eyes. Alisz had once told her of the dream she used to have as a child, where she was an old man out fishing on the ocean. A large and powerful wave swelled up over the boat and she was swept away. "And to this day, my fear of water runs deep," Alisz had said. It was difficult for Lilli to picture Alisz as an old man. Such a strange story, but there were many strange things about Alisz. It was what Lilli loved most about her, and also why she must not speak of these things to Vater. He accepted Alisz's work as a midwife and healer…but there was so much more about Alisz, things she knew Vater would not approve of.

Alisz took some cleansing breaths as she clutched fast to Lilli. When she had finally gained her composure, her expression softened. She looked down at Lilli, soaked with water.

"Oh dear. You do look a fright," she said and suddenly burst into laughter.

Lilli moved away from Alisz. "Then you are not angry?" she said. She shouldn't have wandered so far; Alisz had warned her not to.

"How could I be angry with you, dear, sweet lily-of-the-valley? Come, let us collect our things. It is time to go home."

# CHAPTER FIVE

"**I**T SAYS HERE THAT NETTLE IS NOT GOOD WHEN EATEN RAW as it is much too harsh, but when the new shoots are cooked it will purge the stomach of illness," said Alisz, reading from one of the pages in her stillroom book. "I wonder if this would be an effective remedy for Frau Becker?" She flipped through several more pages. "It says here that fennel is also good for digestion. As is dandelion."

Lilli knew not to disturb Alisz when she was looking for a remedy, a process that sometimes took a good deal of time. Alice liked to talk out loud when searching through the book. Through listening to her ramblings, Lilli had learned countless things. Many herbs had the same medicinal properties as others. Choosing the right one took care and should not be done in haste. Lilli stood on the stool that Alisz had given her when she first started helping out in the stillroom. She was ten now, and nearly tall enough to work at the table without it. But the added height filled her with confidence. Perhaps one day she would be as tall as Alisz.

"This—this is the recipe we shall use," said Alisz, touching the page. "The wormwood will work well for our patient. Frau Becker has a delicate constitution." Alisz always stressed the importance in considering the entire person and not just one symptom.

"But wormwood is for cleansing," said Lilli. Each spring they drank wormwood tea. Alisz insisted. Hildegard von Bingen, an esteemed healer and mystic in the twelfth century, wrote about cleansing the mind, body, and spirit in the spring. Alisz always followed her teachings.

"You are correct, Lilli, but do not forget that every herb has several uses. That is why it is difficult to remember them all, and why we must turn to the book for guidance."

"I am sorry," said Lilli. She should not have questioned Alisz's knowledge.

"Do not be sorry, Lilli. It is good to question if you do not understand something, and equally good to ask for an explanation. It is how we learn. Promise me you will never be shy when it comes to asking questions."

It sounded like a simple promise, but it was not always easy to ask questions, as Lilli found out the day of Frau Wagner's delivery. It was the first birth she had attended. There had been much she did not understand and countless questions that begged for answers, but she remained silent, doing only what Alisz instructed her to do.

Afterward, Alisz praised Lilli's natural instinct for offering comfort. "You were most helpful today," she said. "This is Frau Wagner's tenth child. She is not always in the best spirits when another baby arrives." Lilli didn't mean to laugh, but she couldn't help herself. Alisz was right. Frau Wagner had proven to be most disagreeable, yelling as she hurled objects when Herr Wagner suddenly burst into the room.

"You, dear Lilli, are learning quickly. Soon you will be as knowledgeable as I," said Alisz as they walked homeward that day. Lilli knew Alisz was being too generous. There was so much more to learn. It would take many years.

"One day our Lilli will be a respected midwife and a revered healer," Mutter had said to Vater that day. For all those times in the past when he'd grumbled about Lilli's alliance with Alisz, he seemed slightly pleased when Mutter said this, but that pleasure lasted only a short time.

∽

Beneath the velvety blanket of night, Alisz and Lilli trod quietly through the moonlit meadow. Lilli knew that some plants had to be grown in secret, but this was the first time she'd gone with Alisz to help out in her hidden garden. Before they left that evening, Alisz lit candles, asking the Goddess to bless the seeds they were to plant so they would shoot up strong and sturdy come spring.

Mutter had not wanted Lilli to go out into the night. "Alisz should not have asked," she said.

"Do not blame Alisz," Lilli had pleaded. "If I am to learn healing, I must learn it all. I will be careful and so will Alisz. The cloak of darkness will shield us."

Mutter had uneasily agreed. And now, guided by a cluster of stars above them, Alisz trekked toward their destination in silence. Lilli followed closely behind. The diminished light made the distant landscape appear eerie, and Lilli suddenly feared someone might be following them. Some people believed that witches used certain plants to give them supernatural powers, and that a witch's ointment made from these plants would give them the ability to fly through the night sky, of all things. A ridiculous notion, but it was why Alisz had to grow these plants in secret. If the right person found them growing in her garden, she would be accused of practising witchcraft. While she hid the mandrake beneath large, leafy plants near her home, the garden would only allow her to hide so many. That was why she kept another garden far from home.

"There is nothing to fear," said Alisz as they walked through the meadow. "What lies in the shadows is only your imagination." Lilli pulled in a deep breath and carried onward, determined not to allow her imagination to rule her. Her place was by Alisz's side. It was only right for her to help. It was all part of the teachings she would one day need to know.

"We are here," Alisz finally announced. She set her handbasket down at the edge of the garden, warning Lilli to watch where she stepped. Crouching low to the ground, she removed a bag of henbane seeds from the basket. "We must work quickly," she said, untying the bag.

High above, the hunter's moon provided enough light to work by. Lilli fashioned small furrows in the ground while Alisz dropped in the seeds and covered them. They did the same for the foxglove, sowbread, and cudweed. When the last of the seeds were planted, Alisz turned to the belladonna. The plants were mature and needed to be harvested before they were touched by frost.

"We must be careful," said Alisz as she cut the plant stems. "The berries and leaves are most poisonous."

"Belladonna is in the ointment Herr Werlinger rubs on his knees and ankles," said Lilli as she filled her gathering bag. It was the only treatment that gave him relief from his pain.

"You have learned many things by watching and listening." Again, Alisz sounded pleased with Lilli's knowledge.

When their bags were full, they started back the way they had come. Night surrounded them on their journey home. Lilli's earlier fear of being found out was quieted by the song of a nightingale sitting somewhere in the treetops. She looked toward the sky, hoping she might see a shooting star.

"If only we had brought our broomsticks," whispered Alisz as they walked back through the meadow. "We could use the belladonna to fly home."

"It might be fun to fly and not have to grow wings or feathers," said Lilli. Despite their silly exchange, Lilli couldn't help thinking how delightful it would be to soar through the heavens and look down on the world at night.

"I will walk you home," said Alisz once the belladonna was safely inside the stillroom. But as they neared Lilli's home, they could hear someone stomping toward them in the dark.

Lilli turned toward Alisz. "You must go. Hurry," she whispered as Alisz slipped silently into the dark.

"Lilli. Is that you? Come here at once," boomed Vater's voice into the night.

"I am coming, Vater," she answered, her heart throbbing in her chest. What would she tell him?

"Where have you been, child?" he asked, anger darkening his words.

"I could not sleep. I thought a night stroll might help."

Vater let out a grunt as he followed her toward the house. When she reached for the door latch, he grabbed her hand.

"Be warned, Lilli. I do not want you out at night with that woman. She is not to be trusted. Do you understand?"

"But Vater," whispered Lilli, "if I am to become a healer, I must learn from her. There is no one else." Lilli let out a sigh of relief as Vater released her hand.

### NEW GERMANY, NOVA SCOTIA, 2019

Somehow the book ended up packed away in an old trunk for eight long years; aged and worn, the edges were curled from use, forgotten with time. The year Lilly was thirteen, she and her mother went to the basement in search of newspaper clippings and she found it. At first, she thought it might be one of her mother's scrapbooks, but quickly she saw that she was wrong. On the outside cover, childlike letters formed the name—Lilly.

"That was yours when you were little," said her mother.

"I don't remember it at all," Lilly said, opening the book. She felt disappointed. It was as if she were seeing it for the first time, although something about it felt vaguely familiar. Inside were the crude drawings of a young child.

"A childhood treasure," her mother said. She saved everything, all of Lilly's schoolwork and report cards. She kept every Christmas card she got over the years, and the postcards Great-Uncle Cyrus sent from all over the world.

"A treasure? I'm not so sure about that." Lilly laughed, looking down at the simple crayon drawings. "They aren't very good. I didn't even stay inside the lines."

"You were only five," laughed her mother.

"Alice says that everything has its own story." Lilly stared down at the drawings, wondering what story this book had to tell.

"You certainly told your share of stories when you were drawing in it. We'd tell you not to talk so silly, but you kept insisting that all the stories were real. Such a wild imagination you had. You carried the book around with you day and night. You even slept with it. You didn't want it out of your sight."

Lilly went through the pages slowly, trying to remember back to when she would have drawn the pictures. "What kind of stories did I tell?" she asked, as she struggled to delve deep into her memory.

"Just that you lived in a place across the ocean and you had another book with drawings of plants in it. You said you used to read from it." It was no use. Nothing her mother said sounded even vaguely familiar.

"Guess I liked plants back then too—and the colour blue," she said, looking at the drawings. She laughed at the big blue flower that occupied an entire page. Plants were her thing and had been for as long as she could remember. Her friend Kennedy was into boys and movies, but Lilly thought plants were cool, something Kennedy said made her a little weird to be around.

Lilly continued to studied the flowers and plants and bright colours splashed across the pages. She stopped when she came to a picture of a boat with a large mast.

"This seems strange. A boat in the middle of all these plants."

"Oh, that. Alice told you about her pendant, how a friend gave it to one of her ancestors before sailing across the ocean. You drew that picture the next day and made up stories about coming here on a large ship. You even told Alice that you knew her from before, except she'd had a different name." Lilly and her mother laughed. It sounded so silly, but the strangest part was, Lilly had no recollection of any of it.

"I guess I did have a wild imagination," said Lilly.

Several of the pages at the back of the book were blank. She looked up at her mother. "What happened? Why didn't I finish it?"

"After a while you lost interest. You stopped telling your incredible stories and didn't draw another picture. But I couldn't throw the book away." Her mother smiled.

"Of course not." Lilly was glad she had a mother who did not throw things away.

That night, Lilly opened the book and looked at the drawings. She was curious about the memories she claimed to have had when she was five. Why had they disappeared, never to return? She stared at the pictures, trying hard to find even a small sliver of memory to build upon. But there was nothing. Whatever memories she had hoped to uncover were gone.

She flipped to the empty pages. Why had she stopped drawing so close to the end? Her mother said she'd suddenly lost interest, but that didn't make sense. She obviously loved plants back then as much as she did now. Lilly smiled, thinking of her five-year-old self drawing in the book, and looked once again at the blank pages. An idea struck her then; the book need not be lost in time.

According to Einstein, time is just an illusion anyway. It was something Alice often repeated. Turning to her wildcrafting book, she found a photo of a starflower to replicate. It was one of her favourite plants. There was no reason she couldn't finish the book now. It might be fun. As Lilly pressed the green coloured pencil to the book, a strange tingling began in her fingertips and travelled up her arm. And as the pencil glided across the page, a peaceful sensation warmed her heart.

That night she dreamt about plants and trees, people in long dresses walking beneath a round full moon. And every night after that, the dream returned. And in each of the dreams, there was a woman who looked like her friend Alice Goodwin.

# CHAPTER SIX

WÜRTTEMBERG, 1752

TWILIGHT SLID TOWARD THE HORIZON, PULLING WITH IT soft shades of red and orange and the sacred promise of sunny weather in the days ahead. Planting time would soon be here; Vater would be pleased. Lilli looked out the window. Overhead, thin streaks of clouds slowly shifted, revealing a faded moon barely visible in the evening sky. The moon was only just beginning to wax. In a few weeks it would be round and full. In the nearby rowan tree, a cluster of spring birds gripped tightly to the branches, waiting for night to descend. Dusk was Lilli's favourite part of the day, sitting beside the hearth with Mutter once the chores were done, the outside world quieting down for the night. Sometimes Vater and Friedrich would join them by the fire, but she preferred those times when it was just her and Mutter. Like most nine-year-old boys, Friedrich seldom knew when to be quiet and listen.

The spinning wheel produced a steady rhythm as Mutter pushed an experienced foot against the treadle—up-down, up-down. Lilli had not yet conquered that same masterful technique, but she had only just started spinning last year.

"It is my gift to you," Mutter had said the day Lilli turned thirteen.

"But Mutter..." Lilli was not sure what to say. She had been asking Mutter to teach her how to spin for some time now, but she had always been too busy.

"Perhaps, then, you would like something else," said Mutter, smiling.

"It is the perfect gift," Lilli said as she hurriedly took up Mutter's place by the spinning wheel.

"First you must find the proper rhythm with your foot. You will practise using the pedal whenever you have a spare moment," said Mutter as she watched over Lilli.

"But when will I get to spin the wool?" said Lilli, anxious to feel the spun fibres beneath her touch.

"Once you have mastered this part," said Mutter.

Lilli's foot reached out for the treadle, but as she pushed down, the wheel refused to budge. "But it won't move. There is something wrong," she said. Lilli attempted several more times to make the wheel whirl around. Finally, it began to move, but then stopped suddenly, refusing to turn.

"Sometimes the simple things require the most skill," Mutter said. "You will learn the feel of the treadle beneath your foot until it is second nature."

"But I can't," Lilli said. It had looked so easy all those times Mutter sat spinning by the hearth, the thin fibres of wool slipping freely between her fingers.

"Patience, dear Lilli. You will practise until you have mastered it. Then you will learn to spin the wool. It will take time, but you will learn."

Mutter had been right. Soon Lilli was spinning the wool, but she knew it would take time before she had the same skill as Mutter.

"Come sit by the fire," Mutter said, looking up at Lilli. Taking her place by the hearth, Lilli reached for the wool and began pulling the fibres apart in preparation for spinning. For a brief moment she closed her eyes, soothed by the feel of the newly washed fleece in her hands and the soft shushing of the spinning wheel as it turned around and around.

"You look tired," said Mutter, disturbing the silence Lilli had drifted into. "Did you not sleep well?"

Lilli opened her eyes and smiled warmly. "I slept fine," she said. A few days ago she had come home from Alisz's with a small charm in her pocket. It was to wipe away the nightmares she'd been plagued with lately. But she and Mutter did not dare speak openly about the charm in front of Vater. Lilli would be severely punished if he ever found out. The sight of a charm was something he would not tolerate, especially one that came from Alisz. It might very well be the proof he needed that Alisz was indeed a witch. He had made it very clear, over the years, that he did not trust her.

"I have heard stories concerning Alisz," he would say. "Some of the villagers are talking." Whenever Lilli asked what those stories were, he would not tell.

The door opened and Friedrich dashed inside, bringing with him the remnants of the day he'd spent chasing snakes and capturing bugs in the pond. Puffing and panting, he chose his usual seat beside Lilli, his pink cheeks glowing. Vater was not far behind. Sometimes when he came to the hearth he would ask Lilli to read from the Bible, but she did not expect he would this evening. Recently, he'd been recounting tales of his own, warning about the practise of witchcraft in Württemberg.

A few weeks back, Hans Vogt's barn had burned to the ground, the animals inside barely making their escape. There was talk in the village that it had been the work of witches. A barn would not suddenly catch fire, or so many said. There had been other strange happenings too: fences that had been damaged and grain that had gone sour. Lilli overheard some of the whisperings one day when she and Mutter had gone into the village. People seemed so sure that any bit of misfortune had to have an unearthly cause, that things could not just happen on their own accord. And now, with Walpurgisnacht fast approaching, Lilli suspected their suspicions would be made that much stronger.

"It is impossible to know who the witches are," said Vater one evening. "We must be on our guard at all times." Friedrich hung on his every word while Vater made claims that witches could turn milk sour, strike people dead, and cause diseases. He even stated that they had the ability to raise storms and keep cows from giving milk and some could change their form into that of a hare or a cat at will. "Beware those two—a cat and a hare," said Vater. "Each one can be equally dangerous to mere mortals."

"I saw a hare just yesterday, near the edge of the woods. How do I know if it was a witch?" asked Friedrich, a question Vater did not seem to have the answer to.

Vater's stories told of extraordinary deeds performed by witches, stories that were laced with fear and mystery. They were unbelievable tales, even though Vater would insist they were all true.

"Tell me again about the Brocken, Vater," said Friedrich, taking a ball of wool from the basket. "Is it true that witches fly there on broomsticks?" he asked as he began picking the wool apart.

Nodding his head, Vater began. "There are long-ago stories about such things, a trial in Osnabrück many, many years back. Come closer. I will explain."

Mutter's face displayed her disapproval as Vater moved his chair nearer the hearth, beckoning for Friedrich to do the same. As he placed a stick of wood on the fire, it snapped and crackled.

"Friedrich, my dear," said Mutter, looking up from her spinning, "it is just a story, a fairy tale. No one can fly on a broomstick. Tell him, Karl."

"It is true. Mere mortals cannot jump on broomsticks and take to the sky. The only ones capable of that are witches."

"Karl," Mutter scolded, her foot stopping abruptly on the treadle.

"Marta, this is not for you to interfere. The boy has questions. Curiosity about the world is not a bad thing."

"But—"

Vater's icy stare sent a silent warning to Mutter. She pushed her foot against the treadle and reluctantly went back to her spinning.

"Now, where were we?" said Vater, looking at Friedrich.

"The Brocken, Vater."

"Ah, yes, the Brocken." Vater glanced at Mutter and cleared his throat. "The Brocken is the highest peak in the Harz Mountains, and for that reason the witches go there to meet on Walpurgisnacht to celebrate evil on the last day of Ostermonat. It is a place that cannot be reached by ordinary men."

"The last day of Ostermonat is tomorrow!" said Friedrich gleefully. Lilli's brow creased. Friedrich was too easily influenced by the things he heard. She was sure this Walpurgisnacht was not the grand festivity Vater made it out to be. Württemberg was rich with these stories about witchcraft, but that was all they were—stories, made up to explain the things people did not understand.

"Quiet now, and listen," said Vater, "while I tell you of the trial in Osnabrück, centuries old, yet a powerful story that lives on to this day. One hundred and thirty-three women were accused of practising dark magic on the Witches' Sabbath," said Vater, shaking his finger. "It is said that eight thousand witches were there—eight thousand."

"Did this happen on the Brocken?"

"Yes, this all happened on the Brocken. As I said, it is where they went to celebrate," said Vater, settling comfortably into the story.

Mutter cast him an anxious look, but he ignored her.

"It is said that on the Brocken they drank five cartloads of wine and cast their wicked spells. It was a celebration with loud music, the likes of which has never been heard before or since. And the Devil was there, in the centre of it all, wielding his evil.

"The next day, one hundred and thirty-three witches were burned at the stake. They were part of the celebration that took place the night before, rounded up off the Brocken, they were. It is said that four of the most beautiful witches were spared by the Devil. He reached down and grabbed them into his arms, carrying them away into the chilled night air to keep them from meeting the same fate as the others."

"Why were only one hundred and thirty-three burned when eight thousand were on the Brocken that night?" asked Friedrich. Lilli glanced quickly at Mutter and wondered what Vater now thought of Friedrich and his curiosity.

"That part we are not told," said Vater, clearing his throat. "For that reason, it is not important. The important part to remember is that one hundred and thirty-three were stopped in their witchly tracks from spreading their evil in the world."

It was difficult to tell if Vater's answer had satisfied Friedrich. His face gave little indication. He sat quiet for a time, picking the wool, but then suddenly looked up. "Do the witches still gather at the Brocken, Vater?"

"They can gather wherever they wish—the Brocken or even here in Württemberg."

Friedrich's eyes grew large. Lilli only wished Vater would not fill her brother's head with such nonsense. If people refused to stop telling these stories, they would live on forever. There would never be an end to their fear.

Seeing Friedrich's interest, Vater continued. "It is why to this day, when the sun sets low on the last day of Osnabrück, the Easter month, we still gather to light the fires and make loud noises—all to drive the witches away. To keep us safe for another year."

"It is a good story," said Friedrich, smiling.

Vater nodded. "It is more than just a story. And it is important for you see these things for yourself. A story is not always enough. These things you need to experience. It is why I have decided that this year, you will come with me on Walpurgisnacht to help chase away evil."

"I will?" said Friedrich, jumping from his chair, sending the ball of wool tumbling across the floor.

Mutter abandoned her spinning. "Karl, no. He is but a child. It is no place for him."

"The boy is old enough," said Vater firmly. "He will come with me. Together we will help keep this family safe."

"It is something I cannot allow. This family is perfectly safe. There is no need for you to involve Friedrich."

"Woman," said Vater sternly. "I do not interfere with decisions you have made when it comes to Lilli, and it is not your place to interfere here." With that, Vater stormed from the cottage, taking Friedrich with him.

Lilli scooped up the wool Friedrich had dropped and placed it in the basket beside her. "What decisions?" she whispered.

"It is not important what Vater meant," said Mutter, pushing her foot again the treadle as she went back to her spinning. "Vater wants to justify his own decisions."

"But it concerns me. He said you made decisions. What were they?" said Lilli, setting aside the wool she was picking. Why was Mutter acting so strangely?

"He is speaking about your time spent with Alisz—that is all. You know he does not trust her." Lately, she had heard Mutter and Vater arguing. Vater said she was spending far too much time at Alisz's, that she was shirking her chores at home.

"In time, our Lilli will become a respected healer," Mutter would say. "You know full well that to learn all there is to know will take years."

Mutter went to the window now and peered out into the dusk.

"I fear what will happen to Friedrich should he go out on Walpurgisnacht with Vater. It may not be easy to reassure him that Vater is misguided in his thinking, especially when he sees the others there with him."

"I know, Mutter," said Lilli. "We will do what we can to undermine Vater's influence. It will not be easy."

*I will pray for the Goddess to help us,* thought Lilli as she gazed out the window into the moon's silver face. Even then she was not sure that they could keep Friedrich from believing in witchcraft.

### NEW GERMANY, NOVA SCOTIA, 2019

Lilly wasn't sure what to do about the dreams, or if she should do anything. What she did know was that the dreams made her happy. But what did it all mean? One thing was for certain, she wouldn't tell her parents. They hadn't believed her when she was little, and they wouldn't believe her now. She couldn't tell her friend Kennedy, either—she already thought Lilly was strange because of all the time she spent wildcrafting and learning about plants. Besides, what if these dreams were the same stories she'd made up when she was five?

A part of her didn't know what to believe, if the dreams were of real events or imagined ones. She thought of Alice. Alice was the smartest person she knew. She would tell Alice Goodwin about the dreams on Saturday when they went wildcrafting for coltsfoot. She would explain the strange sensation that had come over her when she'd drawn a starflower in the book. Alice would believe her. She was certain of it. Maybe Alice could even help her figure out what it all meant.

# CHAPTER SEVEN

"**S**LOW DOWN, LITTLE PIGS. THERE IS PLENTY FOR EVERY-one," laughed Lilli the next morning as the chickens fought over the grain she was scattering. Above the fluttering of wings, she could hear Vater speaking to someone. Why wasn't he working in the field, preparing the land for planting? He was usually out at first light. Surely nothing was wrong. When she rounded the corner, she was surprised to see him cutting the branches from a nearby tree and handing them to Friedrich.

"Quickly Mutter, come see. What is Vater doing?" she said, motioning for Mutter to join her.

Mutter sighed when she saw. "He is collecting twigs from the rowan tree. He believes it will ward off witchcraft, that the rowan tree has special powers."

"But he has not done this before." At least not that Lilli could recall.

"You were too young to remember, but there have been times in the past. It has been many years, though, since he has felt the need. He is more frightened these days. All the strange happenings of late. He believes it is his duty to protect this family."

"Bring them along," Vater said to Friedrich as he marched past Lilli and Mutter. With his arms filled with the freshly cut sticks, Friedrich hurried to keep up.

Ever since Herr Vogt's barn burned down, Württemberg had become riddled with suspicion. Old fears were being reignited and long-forgotten superstitions talked about once again. Suddenly people worried that every small mishap might be the work of witches. Was witchcraft really making a resurgence in Württemberg? Many, like Vater, believed it was possible, and Lilli feared what that would mean for all of them.

"Why are you doing that?" asked Friedrich as Vater began hanging some of the branches over the doorway.

"I have already told you. The rowan branches will cure a house of witchcraft."

Friedrich looked up at Vater with wide eyes. "Is our house bewitched?" Vater did not answer but continued with his task.

"It is a precaution," he said when he finished securing the branches above the doorway. "One can never be too safe *or* too sure. I have seen enough in my day to know. Now, bring the rest inside."

"Karl," sighed Mutter. "Is this truly necessary?"

"This is not your concern, Marta. Come now, Friedrich, bring the rowan." Mutter and Lilli followed close behind.

"You must stop him," whispered Lilli as Vater continued to hang more rowan branches about the house. Mutter shook her head. There was nothing she could do. When the last of the branches were in place, Vater presented Friedrich with a small wooden cross. Friedrich smiled as he wrapped his hand around it. Lilli wished Vater wouldn't fill her brother's head with such nonsense. Friedrich was young and eagerly believed the things he was told.

"We will need to protect ourselves. Keep the cross with you at all times, Friedrich."

"I will," said Friedrich, tucking it into his waistband.

When Vater held out two crudely carved crosses to Mutter and Lilli, they both refused.

"I may not be able to stop you from putting rowan branches inside our dwelling," said Mutter firmly, "but I will not be a part of this, and neither will Lilli." Lilli was afraid that Vater might order them to take the crosses, but he didn't. He pulled back his shoulders and looked down at Friedrich.

"Come now, Friedrich," he said with a grunt. "At least someone in this family listens. We will fill the wagon with sticks and wood to take with us tonight."

Shortly after the evening meal, Vater hitched the ox to the wagon. He had plans to meet up with some of the other villagers.

"Will you not change your mind about taking Friedrich?" Mutter said. "He is but a boy. It may not be safe for him."

"It will be safe," said Vater as he removed two ox bells from an old trunk. He gave them to Friedrich and told him to climb onto the wagon. Friedrich scurried outside; the bells in his hands rattled. Lilli wondered what they planned to do with them.

Vater looked at Mutter one last time. "Do not worry. I will see to it that Friedrich is safe," he said closing the door.

Lilli stood in the doorway with Mutter as the silhouette of the ox and wagon was slowly swallowed up by the twilight.

"Where will they go to meet for this Walpurgisnacht, Mutter?" Lilli had been trying to think of places. She imagined it to be a secluded spot, some clearing in the woods perhaps, the night air filled with the shouts and cries from men and boys. A place where flames would have the freedom to leap and frolic, all with the hopes of chasing away some nonexistent evil they believed in.

"They go to a secret place," said Mutter. "Vater never says where, nor do I ask. It is barbaric, a practise old as time. I have asked him not to partake, many times I have asked. All he says is that he has been going since he was a boy and he will not stop now. He believes he is protecting us, Lilli."

The branches from the rowan tree scraped the side of the house in the breeze, a reminder to Lilli that their home was now protected from witches.

"Come inside," Mutter urged. "There is nothing you can do."

"Soon," said Lilli as she wrapped her arms around herself. The soft clank of ox bells in the distance reminded her of the times Vater would travel to a neighbouring village, a journey that sometimes took him away for an entire day. She would wait by the gate for the sound of bells telling of his return, and would run the narrow path to meet him. Vater would stop the wagon and reach down for her, placing her in the seat beside him. He'd tell her about the places he'd been and all the wondrous sights he had witnessed. Sometimes he would bring small gifts. There was never any talk of witches. If only things could go back to the way they once were.

# CHAPTER EIGHT

"**I HAVE MADE UP MY MIND. I AM GOING TO SEE THIS** Walpurgisnacht for myself," said Lilli, closing the front door. If she found their meeting place, she might discover a way to put a stop to it. Perhaps she could send positive energy into their gathering and inject light into their hearts and minds. Alisz often said that only light can chase away the darkness. They might forget their fear of witchcraft and all would be well again.

"Lilli, no, this is not for women or girls. It is no place for you. Should you be discovered..."

"When the moon is full, I go out at night and meet with Alisz to harvest plants and roots," she reminded Mutter. "I am always careful. Tonight will be no different."

"Then I will come with you."

"No, Mutter. What if Vater returns and finds us both gone? What would you tell him?" Touching Mutter gently on the arm, she added with a smile, "You do not need to worry. The Night Goddess will protect me."

"Lilli, you must stop this talk about Goddesses. We are good Protestant people. We follow the word of God."

"But Alisz says—"

"Alisz is not right about everything. Perhaps she does not believe the words in the Bible, but we do."

A rattle came at the door before Lilli had time to put on her wrap and slip out of the house. She stopped suddenly, sending Mutter a puzzled look. Who could possibly be outside? A muffled voice called out for someone to please hurry. Fumbling with the latch, Lilli unfastened the door. Herr Ludwig was waiting outside.

"Whatever is the matter?" Lilli asked, sensing that something was terribly wrong. It was not like Herr Ludwig to show up this time of evening without warning. Actually, it was not like Herr Ludwig to show up at their door at all. The Ludwigs had moved to the area a few months back. Mutter and Lilli had gone to welcome them to Württemberg. Frau Ludwig had returned their visit in early April, but Herr Ludwig had never once come calling.

"Please, Fräulein," he blurted out. "You are needed. The midwife, Alisz, says you must come." The wave of worry across his face spoke to Lilli's heart. Frau Ludwig's time was coming near and Alisz had gone to check on her several times over the past week.

"The baby should be resting," Alisz had told Lilli, "getting ready for its journey, but instead it kicks like an angry mule. It is a very strange thing. This child will be headstrong and will cause its parents much worry."

"We must move quickly, then," Lilli said to Herr Ludwig as Mutter handed Lilli her wrap.

"Stay safe. I will say prayers for everyone," Mutter whispered, hugging Lilli.

"Thank you, Mutter. It will help greatly if you continue to think positive thoughts." Lilli paused when she saw the look Mutter gave her. "Is that not what prayers are, after all—positive thoughts?" she added softly.

In the years since the Wagner child was born, Lilli had attended several other births when Alisz sent for her help, and each birth had been a miraculous event with cries of pain and joy intertwined. Every time, Alisz had taken the wiggling bundle outside to greet the Earth Goddess before resting the child safely inside its mother's waiting arms. But Lilli could not shake the idea that something was different this time. There had never been this sense of urgency in the past.

"Alisz said you will need to bring some mutterkorn. She said that you would know where to find it," Herr Ludwig added as Lilli kept in step with his broad strides. Mounting his mare, he reached down to help her up onto the horse's back.

Lilli did not need any special powers to tell her that Frau Ludwig's delivery was not going well. She was familiar with the different herbs Alisz took with her for deliveries—raspberry leaf, birth root. Often times she burnt juniper berries and twigs on the hearth to purify the room, but never mutterkorn. Mutterkorn was used to speed up a birth, but only under exceptional circumstances. It is why Alisz did not carry it with her. So far as Lilli knew, she had never had reason to use it.

"I will need to stop at Alisz's cottage," Lilli said, grasping Herr Ludwig's hand. "Herr Ludwig," she whispered softly before climbing up onto the horse. "Do not worry. Alisz is knowledgeable. Your wife and child will be fine."

"I hope you are right," he said, helping Lilli onto the back of his mare. Lilli clung tightly to Herr Ludwig as they raced through the rugged terrain. By the time they reached Alisz's small cottage, the light had been drained from the day. There was only the glow from the full moon to steer her.

Quickly entering the stillroom, Lilli stopped just inside the door. Moonlight reached inside the cottage, offering barely enough light to distinguish the objects in her path.

"I store the birthing powder on the very top shelf, at the back. It is only to be used as a last resort," Alisz had once told her, stressing that if used incorrectly, it could bring about deadly results. "There are many herbs that have the power to kill or cure. You must treat them all with respect. These are the things you will learn over time."

With help from the moon's guiding hand, Lilli made her way to the herbs and roots lined up neatly on the shelves.

"Hurry, Fräulein," Herr Ludwig cried from outside. Lilli could hear the horse moving about restlessly.

"I will not be long," she answered. Careful not to bump any of the jars, Lilli removed the one she was certain contained the birthing powder. She held it up to make sure it was the correct shape and size. Moving out from the shelves, she set it on the table and removed the lid. She took a quick whiff of the contents, recognizing the distinct aroma.

With the jar of birth powder tucked inside her wrap, they hurried off once again into the night. Holding tightly to Herr Ludwig, Lilli closed her eyes and focused her mind on a positive outcome the way Alisz had taught her. She imagined a bright smile spread across Herr Ludwig's face, and Frau Ludwig releasing tears of great joy. She heard the cries of a healthy baby—all this she imagined while feeling a strong joy deep in her heart. She did not open her eyes until the mare's strides slowed. The wind whistled through the tree branches as Herr Ludwig dismounted and helped Lilli to the ground. She could hear Frau Ludwig's cries all the way outside.

"You must stay out and let Alisz do her work," she told Herr Ludwig when he attempted to follow Lilli inside.

"But Fräulein—"

"This is not the place for men," she said as she closed the door in his face. Candles lit the room, offering a dim amount of light. The tangled scents of lavender and peppermint hung heavy in the air. The herbs were sprinkled over the floor to help calm the mother, but from the sounds that were coming from the next room, Frau Ludwig was anything but calm. She was howling like a wounded animal.

"Alisz, I am here," Lilli called out.

"Come this way," Alisz answered from the adjourning room.

Removing the small jar of mutterkorn from her wrap, Lilli hurried to where Frau Ludwig lay writhing in pain. Her forehead was wet with perspiration, her hair flat against her head. Her brow was creased and her eyes were squeezed tightly together. Alisz was by her side and Frau Ludwig was gripping Alisz's hands so tightly her fingers were white. Alisz looked up expectantly. "You found it," she said, as Lilli held the small jar out to her.

Alisz released her hand from Frau Ludwig's and hurriedly took the birth powder from Lilli. "We need just a small amount," she said. Frau Ludwig let out an agonizing cry, screaming for Alisz to hurry and make the pain stop.

"Will Frau Ludwig be all right?" Lilli whispered.

"It has been a long labour. Now go, sit with her while I prepare the powder. Reassure her that all will be well."

"But will the mutterkorn work?" Lilli whispered in desperation as Frau Ludwig's cries turned into whimpers.

"Let us pray so." The look on Alisz's face caused a strange sensation in Lilli. What if Alisz could not help Frau Ludwig? What if she died giving birth? She knew it was within the realm of possibility. Such things could not always be prevented, no matter what measures were taken. Alisz was always careful, but was there room for mistakes?

But no, she would not allow her mind to explore these possibilities. She would remain positive no matter how bleak the situation might seem at the moment. The birth powder would do its job. It had to.

# CHAPTER NINE

THE MUTTERKORN DID NOT TAKE LONG TO WORK. FRAU Ludwig looked hesitant when Alisz mixed it with a little water and held it up to her trembling lips.

"This baby needs to come out," Alisz said firmly when Frau Ludwig resisted. "It is tired and you are tired. I will not lose either of you. Do you understand?"

Frau Ludwig shook her head and begged once again for an end to her pain. She swallowed the birth powder between contractions, relaxing momentarily when Alisz laid a gentle hand on the side of her face.

"This will increase your pains and bring that baby out," said Alisz. "The time is now." Lilli could tell that Alisz was not completely convinced of this herself, but neither of them would voice their misgivings. It was important to remain positive for Frau Ludwig's sake.

Alisz looked directly into Frau Ludwig's eyes. "You must do exactly what I tell you. Are you ready?" she said calmly.

Frau Ludwig howled as the mutterkorn took effect. She screamed and pushed each time Alisz instructed her to. One long, loud wail from Frau Ludwig and the room became hushed except for Frau Ludwig's quiet panting. Lilli waited for the sound of a baby's cry to crack the stillness, but nothing came.

"What is the matter? Is it dead?" Frau Ludwig sounded frantic. Alisz did not answer right away. She removed the phlegm from the baby's mouth and began rubbing its tiny chest and back, coaxing it into drawing a breath.

*Please, oh please,* Lilli silently prayed.

"Let me see," Frau Ludwig wailed as she struggled to observe what Alisz was doing. "Something is wrong. I want to see."

Lilli stroked the sides of Frau Ludwig's head and made shushing noises to comfort her. "Let Alisz to do her work. It will be okay," she whispered, hoping her words would not end up betraying her. She held her breath as she waited for the sounds of a baby crying.

It was not long before a soft mewling could be heard. Weak in the beginning, it slowly gained strength until the walls of the Ludwig dwelling vibrated with the cries of a newborn baby. Frau Ludwig's sobs suddenly turned to laughter. Tears sprang to Lilli's eyes and she joined Frau Ludwig in her mirth. Such a wonderfully joyful sound, when Lilli had secretly feared the worse. Alisz had done it; she had saved both mutter and child!

"Your baby is a girl," said Alisz, beaming a smile of relief and happiness at Frau Ludwig. She, too, could not hold in her glee. When their laughter finally subsided, Alisz wrapped the wiggling bundle in warm blankets. "Does your baby have a name?" she asked.

"Lisette...after Oma," said Frau Ludwig, smiling with out-stretched arms as she waited for Alisz to give her the baby.

"Lisette is a strong name," said Alisz. "She will grow to be a strong woman one day. She will make you proud."

"My baby. I want my baby," said Frau Ludwig as Alisz headed toward the doorway with the child still in her arms.

Alisz smiled and said, "There is something I must do. I will be back shortly."

"Do not worry," Lilli said, gently touching Frau Ludwig's hand. She followed Alisz as she took the newborn child outside, beneath a multitude of stars, and welcomed her into the waiting arms of the Earth Goddess.

"Welcome to the green earth before you, your home for this earthly incarnation. Treat it with the utmost respect and dignity as you travel through her grassy knolls. May you follow your heart as you journey through this path called life, and may you recognize all the blessings that have been placed before you."

Later, as Lilli and Alisz prepared to leave the Ludwigs' home, they stood outside, marvelling at the many stars flickering in the cool night air.

"Do you think the stars hold our destiny?" said Lilli, gazing into the infinite blackness with no beginning and no end.

"I believe we are the ones who hold our own destiny," said Alisz. "We create our lives with every decision we make—good or bad. We are the ones responsible for our own joy and also the ones who bring about our own tears. It might be easy to blame the stars, but that blame would be misspent."

Lilli glanced over at Alisz. She looked to be mesmerized by the night sky, but then she quickly drew in a breath and smiled at her young apprentice.

"You did very well tonight. The outcome could have been far different had you not come," she said. "I could not have done it without your help."

"It was the mutterkorn," said Lilli. "I did not do anything worthy of such praise."

"You helped keep Frau Ludwig calm. I saw how you quieted her. You have a special way about you when it comes to comforting others. It is your special gift."

"You were the one who saved Frau Ludwig and her baby," Lilli reminded her. How could Alisz say otherwise?

"Now come, dear Lilli," said Alisz, smiling. "It is late. We must go home. It has been a long night."

∞

## NEW GERMANY, NOVA SCOTIA, 2019

"How nice that you can remember the stories you made up when you were little," said Alice as they searched along the trail for the bright yellow coltsfoot.

"But what if they're not made-up stories? What if it really happened?" said Lilly. She hoped Alice wouldn't laugh. They'd been friends for a very long time. Alice often listened when Lilly's parents didn't. She was almost like family.

"You would remember these things when you are awake if they had actually happened, not just in your dream state," said Alice in her practical way. She was good at making sense of things that did not always seem logical.

"I know it sounds stupid, but the dream felt real. And when the cinnamon-haired woman looked at me, it was as if I already knew her."

Alice nodded knowingly. "I've read that imagination and memory can become confused. Sometimes we can't distinguish between the two. They're called false memories, and they can seem very real. Perhaps the book triggered these childhood memories of the stories you made up. Hurry, I see a lovely patch of coltsfoot up ahead," said Alice as she beckoned Lilly to follow.

"It seemed so real," said Lilly. Crouching onto the ground close to Alice, she removed her pruning shears and began harvesting the coltsfoot. What if Alice was right? What if the dreams were just her overactive imagination?

Alice smiled. "Don't look so serious, Lilly. Whatever it is you experienced, you should enjoy these wonderful dreams. Who knows, maybe one day you'll become a great storyteller."

"Maybe," said Lilly, feeling a bit let down. She'd been sure that if anyone would believe her, it would be Alice.

"Be careful," warned Alice as Lilly gingerly made her way further down the steep embankment where the coltsfoot grew. "If you fall in the river, I won't be able to save you." Lilly looked at Alice and laughed.

"Little babies can swim. Don't you think it's time you could too?"

"I must have drowned in a past life," laughed Alice, something she said whenever Lilly tried to talk her into taking some swimming lessons.

When Lilly got home, she spent the afternoon at her computer searching out information on false memories. When she read that people can remember events differently from the way they actually happened, or even remember things that never happened at all, she decided that Alice was probably right. She had imagined these stories of long ago when she was small, and now was confusing them with her own memories. It was why the dream had seemed so real.

That night, for the first time, fire leapt into Lilly's dreams.

# CHAPTER TEN

WÜRTTEMBERG, 1752

THE MOON GLOWED STEADILY DOWN AS LILLI AND ALISZ slipped quietly through the forest. The safe arrival of the Ludwig child had warmed Lilli's heart, but now, in the quiet of the night, her thoughts turned to Vater and Friedrich. She had hoped to follow them this evening, to see this Walpurgisnacht. But that was not to be the case. Alisz had needed her help.

"The birth of a child is always a miraculous thing, and this one even more so," said Alisz, breaking the quiet that had settled between them. When Lilli failed to respond, she asked what was wrong.

"Perhaps we should not be out on the Witches' Eve," said Lilli in a tone that indicated her displeasure.

"The Witches' Eve?" Alisz looked over at her young apprentice. "What do you mean?"

Lilli slowed her pace and sighed. "It is Vater. He has taken Friedrich with him tonight."

"Yes, of course, you mean Walpurgisnacht."

"Not only that, he put rowan branches all around our home today—inside *and* out. Mutter could not stop him. He even gave Friedrich a cross...to keep with him at all times. 'It will protect you from witches,' he said."

Alisz reached out for Lilli's hand. "You must try to understand. Fear can be all-consuming."

"I do not need to understand; nor will I listen to excuses," said Lilli, stomping away. Vater's ignorance would one day bring them all grief. He would keep this fear of witchcraft going. Friedrich would grow up not knowing any difference. He would pass this fear of witchcraft to his children and his children's children. It would never stop. Alisz was far too willing to see the good in everyone. Why did she have to be so understanding of others?

"My dear Lilli, you need rest. This day has been a difficult one. In the morning, things will look better. I promise."

"That is where you are wrong, Alisz. Morning will come and nothing will have changed. Vater will be the same stubborn man tomorrow as he was today and all the days before that."

Alisz draped an arm around Lilli's shoulder. "Have faith," she whispered.

Lights glowed in the distance as they continued the walk homeward. The farther they walked into the night, the brighter the lights became. Lilli had never seen anything like it, soft shades of gold and orange stretched out across the darkness.

"Is it the Night Goddess?" she asked.

"The Night Goddess rides her chariot across the sky, dropping stars and bringing a path of darkness with her. This light is not the Night Goddess's doing. I am afraid this is a light made by man."

"Walpurgisnacht!" gasped Lilli, feeling a sudden chill in the air. She looked at Alisz. "I want to see."

"Then we must move swiftly," said Alisz as they hurried toward the glowing light.

"Stay back," warned Alisz as they located the origin of the lights on the other side of the forest. Loud sounds pulsed into the night air as they drew nearer the gathering place. They hid behind a wagon to watch.

Lilli brought her hands to her ears. The noise was near deafening. She could feel the heat from the large bonfire. More sticks were added to the fire as the flames danced and leaped. Each crack from a whip made Lilli flinch. Men and boys were beating the ground with sticks; others were ringing ox bells. How could so many believe? Lilli did not recognize any of the villagers and wondered if Vater and Friedrich were still among them. The sounds turned to chants that pulsated and throbbed. Her heart beat in unison. She stood mesmerized as if under a spell.

"Lilli," whispered Alisz, tapping her on the shoulder. She turned back toward Alisz. Light from the flames illuminated her face. There was a look in her eyes. Lilli could not tell if it was fear or anger or sadness or a mixture of all three.

"Come. This is no place for us. We must go," urged Alisz. "We must go now."

∾

"Lilli, I understand you were there for the birth of the Ludwig child," Vater said one evening not long after Walpurgisnacht. Small sparks from the hearth sprayed into the air as he stirred the fire. The evening was cool for May and the fire felt inviting.

"Yes, Vater, the Ludwigs have a strong, healthy girl," said Lilli, looking up from the wool she was picking.

"Why do you ask, Karl?" said Mutter, stopping her spinning.

"There is word that all is not right with the child, that she cries day and night," he said.

"That is nothing unusual. Some children do, to the chagrin of their poor parents. You must remember how Friedrich used to wail at bedtime—for many months, he wailed until he finally settled down, and then it was almost impossible to get him up in the morning," said Mutter.

"I *do* remember that," said Vater nodding. "It is just that..." He paused for a few seconds, catching Lilli's glance. "Is it true what they say, that the child was born with a tooth?"

"A tooth? I know nothing about a tooth," said Lilli. How could a baby possibly be born with a tooth? She had never heard of such a thing.

"Some are saying it is true, that Herr Ludwig has said so himself." Vater got up from his chair and began pacing the length of the kitchen.

"What is it?" asked Mutter.

"I do not know. It is a delicate situation. Some are even saying it is a sign."

"A sign of what, Karl? You are talking about an innocent baby."

"Some are saying perhaps not so innocent."

"That is plain ridiculous."

"I cannot stop the things that are being said."

"Perhaps so, but you do not have to repeat what you hear." Vater seemed oblivious of the sound of annoyance in Mutter's voice. "Did all go well with the birth, Lilli? Did anything curious happen?" he asked.

"I saw nothing unusual," said Lilli. She knew better than to tell Vater any of the details, how Alisz had to give Frau Ludwig mutterkorn or that the baby did not breathe right away. He might misinterpret these things, make them into something more than they were. For certain, these others he spoke of would.

"That is good," he said with a stingy smile. "Others have encouraged me to inquire. They know of your work with Alisz, that you were present at the birth of the Ludwig child."

Lilli could hear Mutter and Vater whispering long into the night.

"There is more to this than you are telling," said Mutter in a low voice.

"Marta, the child was born on Walpurgisnacht, the Witches' Eve. That in itself—"

"Means nothing," said Mutter. "It is simply a coincidence, a happenstance."

"Perhaps so, but to some in Württemberg it is cause for concern. It is being said that she is a witch's child, that perhaps Frau Ludwig is not who she appears to be."

"How can they say such things about an innocent child?" said Mutter.

"I agree, a baby can do no harm."

"Then you must tell this to the ones who have raised concern. Someone must speak out."

"I cannot very well do that, Marta, as you well know. There is also Frau Ludwig."

"Frau Ludwig has done nothing."

"Perhaps," said Vater. "And now it is time to sleep. We can discuss this later."

$\infty$

"Vater, Frau Ludwig is not a witch, nor is her baby," said Lilli to Vater the next morning. It was ridiculous to even think such a thing.

"You need not be concerned, Lilli. This is a matter for adults. It has nothing to do with you," he said with a small smile.

But Vater's words did little to reassure Lilli. Should the wrong person's voice be heard and believed, no one in Württemberg would be safe.

$\infty$

## NEW GERMANY, NOVA SCOTIA, 2019

The dream always starts out the same. Lilly is walking through the forest or across an open meadow. She's not in New Germany. She doesn't know where she is. The landscape, the trees and plants look different from what she's used to. The cinnamon-haired woman is also in the dream. She is speaking a different language. They both are. Sometimes they are together, laughing as they forage for plants. The next moment Lilly is standing beside a river, looking at her refection. Smiling, she waves and the reflection waves back. Lilly is peaceful and happy. The sun is warm. Birds flitter past, their songs piercing the air around her. She calls out to the woman in her dream. "Please, wait for me. Please wait." But the cinnamon-haired woman keeps walking as if she doesn't understand. Lilly must run to catch up.

But then the dream suddenly shifts and the sky becomes dark. A shadowy figure in a chariot crosses the night sky, dropping stars one by one. A cloak of darkness is being pulled behind the chariot. Now Lilly is running in the dark. Not away from danger, but toward it. She doesn't stop. She can't. Her feet won't let her. They lead her down a well-beaten path. She stops suddenly, her lungs screaming for air. In the distance, a house is engulfed by fire. The happy, giggly feeling she felt by the riverbank is gone, and for the first time the dream brings fear.

# CHAPTER ELEVEN

WÜRTTEMBERG, 1752

"LILLI!! COME HERE. COME HERE AT ONCE!"

Fear leapt to the bottom of Lilli's heart as she and Mutter shared a worried look.

"What is this, Lilli? Tell me what this is!" Anger sat on Vater's tongue, ready to burst into something severe if the answer she gave did not satisfy him.

"Go," whispered Mutter, gently pushing her toward the doorway. "Quickly."

Scurrying toward the sound of Vater's voice, Lilli pulled in a quick breath. She stopped the moment she saw what he was holding. The charm Alisz had given her weeks ago hung down between his pinched fingers. Suspicion rested between the weathered lines on his face as he waited for her to answer.

"Where did you find it?" she asked.

"It was over there on the floor, near the hearth." Had he opened the bag, seen the herbs and the lock of hair tucked inside? Lilli begged her heart to stop thumping so wildly. Vater would hear and know something was wrong. She could not imagine how the charm had gotten out from beneath the straw tick she slept on at night. She had always been so careful.

"Is it yours, Lilli? Did you bring it home from that woman's house? Tell me. Did you?"

Lilli struggled to find her voice. She needed to choose her words with care.

"I have asked you a question," said Vater, waiting for Lilli to speak.

Words refused to form. If Vater decided that she was lying, he might declare Alisz a witch. What more he would do, she did not dare think about. *Thou shall not suffer a witch to live*—Lilli had heard Vater repeat those words from the Bible many times. The strange happenings taking place in Württemberg this past while had made him wary of nearly everyone.

"Answer me, Lilli," Vater continued.

"It is only flower petals," she said, finally forcing the words loose. Courageously, she reached out and snatched the cloth bag from his fingers.

"Flower petals?" he grunted, straightening his shoulders.

"I keep it in my room for the scent. Lavender is the sweetest, as is lily of the valley. A mouse must have dragged it out here." She gave it a quick sniff as a flaming forest of fear burned inside her. "But it is no good now. The smell is gone," she said, tossing it carelessly into the hearth. The fire greedily devoured it. In no time at all, it was gone.

Vater continued to eye her suspiciously. Lilli prayed he would accept her explanation and go about his work for the day.

"You are not to bring these things into the house again, Lilli. Do you hear me? People would not understand. Even I would question such a thing…even I."

"Yes, Vater," she said, casting her eyes downward at the floor. It was always her best defence against Vater's anger.

"Why can you not behave like others girls your age? You should be cooking and spinning wool, not roaming about in the woods gathering up flower petals," said Vater, heading toward the door. Stopping short, he turned back toward her. "Your work to become a midwife and healer is one thing, but this is not the same. I do not want to find anything like this again. Do you understand me?"

"Yes, Vater," Lilli whispered.

Mutter hurried to Lilli's side as soon as the door closed behind Vater. "You will need to be more careful, Lilli. You know what Vater is like," she said. "If he ever suspected, even for a moment..."

Lilli's arms offered little comfort as she wrapped them around herself. "I know, Mutter," she whispered quietly. "I know."

### NEW GERMANY, NOVA SCOTIA, 2019

A huge bonfire is burning deep in a forest. A group of people surround it, throwing more wood into the flames. Lilly can feel the heat from the fire, her heart matching the chants that boom out into the darkness. Flames dance against the night sky, spitting sparks into the air, into the shadows. Large plumes of smoke climb higher and higher. There is shouting in the distance, people are beating the ground with sticks and ringing bells. Voices are chanting. Lilly can't understand what they are saying. The words drone on and on into the night.

She tosses and turns in sleep. Winding and twisting, the sound burrows deeper and deeper as the chanting continues. She is watching from a distance, a silent observer, yet at the same time a part of the scene she is witnessing as if there are two of her.

Someone grabs her hand and they run through the darkened night. When they finally stop running, the cinnamon-haired woman turns and looks directly at Lilly. She smiles.

A sound lingers into the night—a foreign word. One Lilly has never heard before. *Walpurgisnacht.*

# CHAPTER TWELVE

WÜRTTEMBERG, 1752

"**V**ATER DISCOVERED THE CHARM YOU GAVE ME." THE words spilled out of Lilli like flax seeds from an open hand.

Alisz stopped turning the pages of her book and looked up. "When was this?"

"Two days ago."

"And what did you tell him?"

"I told him it was lavender, that I like the scent under my head at night. I burnt it before he had time to look inside. There was no other way." Lilli saw a seed of worry sprouting in Alisz's eyes. "Do not fret, Alisz. Everything is fine. He did not suspect a thing."

"And the dream—has it returned?" Concern brushed the tips of its fingers across Alisz's face, grazing the delicate lines that marked the sides of her mouth and eyes.

"Last night. It woke me up again," Lilli reluctantly admitted. Mutter had heard her gasping in the middle of the night and hurried to her side.

"Shush...you will wake Vater," she had whispered, rocking Lilli in the dark.

"I will make you another charm," Alisz said, quickly flipping through her book.

Lilli plucked some dried chamomile from the stem, feigning indifference about the dream. She did not dare bring another charm into the house. Should Vater discover something again, he would not be so forgiving.

"I am fine for now. Besides, it is just a dream."

"And one that has haunted you for many weeks. I have not forgotten."

When the nightmares began to occur every night, Lilli had begged Alisz for a charm to make them stop.

"I am not even certain such charms exist," she had said.

"But they are in the book. I've seen them myself," Lilli had eagerly reminded her.

"I will look," Alisz had said. "But I will not make any promises."

Lilli had watched in earnest as Alisz flipped through the pages of the book until she came to the section marked *Charms*.

"Here is one that might just work," Alisz had said thoughtfully. She'd filled a small cloth sack with herbs and roots. Cutting a lock of Lilli's hair, she'd added it to the bag.

"Place it under your head at night," Alisz said that day, pulling the string tight. She then told Lilli some words to whisper before bedtime—a tiny prayer to release the dream's hold on her. "And if this does not work, we will have to look for some other solution." But another solution had not been necessary. With the charm beneath Lilli's head at the night, the dream had not returned.

"Keep looking for your remedy, Alisz, and do not worry about me or my dreams. I will be fine," said Lilli, sending a smile Alisz's way. She had no right to mention her dream today of all days, with the Hafner child so sick. Vater always said Lilli was a selfish child.

"Are you certain?" Alisz asked. "It would not take long to find. Perhaps when I am through here."

"I am used to the dream by now. Please, do not worry. Besides, I have been thinking of ways to make the dream go away."

"Without a charm, how would you accomplish this?"

Lilli smiled. "We are more powerful than we give ourselves credit for," she said, repeating Alisz's own words.

"I see you have been listening," said Alisz, smiling as she returned to the pages of her book.

Lilli picked up a sprig of chamomile. Alisz had once told her that dreams were messages of the soul. Lilli had been trying to figure out what message the dream had for her, but so far she had been unsuccessful. Her plan now was to take control of the dream while she was sleeping and drive it away. It would take courage on her part and a strong knowing for her to recognize the dream when she entered it, something she had not yet been able to do. She had not told Alisz about her plan, as she was determined to do it on her own.

The chamomile stripped bare, Lilli placed the stem on the table and took another sprig from the basket. Alisz raised an eyebrow. Realizing she had not managed to convince Alisz that all was well, Lilli tried again.

"What if the dream is just a memory from a past life, a wisp of remembrance from another time and place? You have said so yourself. We have all lived before, through many lifetimes."

Alisz often spoke about the continuation of life, of birth and death and rebirth. She stopped abruptly, nodding while considering Lilli's words. "There *is* a thin veil between this life and another, and there are times when the veil is the thinnest of all. You could be right. Perhaps this is where the dream originates from." A smile stretched across her face just then. "How did you become so wise?"

"I had the good fortune to have a most patient and wise teacher," said Lilli, playfully tossing a small sprig of chamomile Alisz's way.

"Well then, oh wise one, we must also keep in mind that not every dream is meant for the dreamer. Sometimes our dreams are meant for someone else."

Lilli agreed. "It has been some time now and nothing has happened."

She was aware of Alisz's own dream of a fox darting among the low shrubs and undergrowth—a dream that had come back to her several times over the past few months. A running fox spoke of deception; someone close to the dreamer is capable of trickery or betrayal. But the people closest to Alisz came seeking her help. They trusted her to heal them. Would someone she knew really betray her? It seemed impossible to imagine. Perhaps she *was* worried for nothing. Lilli hoped for some sign that would put her mind to rest, one that would tell her that her dream was meaningless.

Alisz's frustration was mounting with each page she turned. She had gone through her book several times, searching for the cure that would heal the Hafner child. The book contained a bounty of knowledge—recipes, cures, charms, snippets of information about the weather and the soil conditions needed for planting, even sketches of the plants Alisz used in her work—squeezed upon each page with no room to spare. Decades of wisdom were inscribed within the book, written by the women in Alisz's family. The empty pages near the back indicated there were more cures still to be discovered.

"When there is a cure for all the ails in this world, the book will be filled," Alisz once said.

"Here. Right here. I found you! Why did I not see you before? I looked upon this page several times already. I am sure of it." Alisz pressed her finger against the aged parchment and leaned in closely.

"Why were you hiding from me like that? It is not nice to hide when I am looking for you, and certainly not when someone is ill."

Lilli smiled. She would never tire of Alisz's strange ways; the talks she gave to the plants in her garden; the way she thanked every growing thing she plucked from the earth.

"Come, Lilli. We will need mugwort, elderberry, and liverwort," she said, reading through the list. Laying aside the chamomile, Lilli hurried toward the shelves.

"Some fever grass, too. I have used this remedy only once, and that was many years ago. It is powerful medicine and only to be used in the most serious of cases."

Alisz looked down at the book again. "We will also need bear fat. It has strong healing properties. Bear fat will make a perfect salve. The Hafner child is as good as cured."

Alisz's feet moved in a delicate dance as hope spiralled about the stillroom for the first time that day. If anyone could cure the Hafner child, it was Alisz. Two times in the past week Frau Hafner had sent her husband to Alisz's back door, each time asking for a new remedy for a mysterious ailment that had stricken their daughter. Nothing seemed to be working. The child was still gravely ill; no one seemed to know the reason why. If Alisz did not find something soon, Lilli feared the child might die, but it was a fear she could not give voice to. Alisz would not allow such ominous thoughts to enter the stillroom.

"We become the thoughts we think each day," Alisz would often say. "So think only happy thoughts, dear Lilli, and leave those sad, gloomy ones outside the door."

Removing a kettle from the wall, Alisz pulled a wooden spoon from the drawer. Directly behind her, glass jars lined the shelves. They were filled with dried plants and roots. Just as Lilli held up the jar containing mugwort, the morning sun burst through the tiny window in the stillroom. Sunbeams reflected off the copper kettles hanging on the walls and danced merrily against the ceiling. Bright radiance spun in all directions as a rainbow of colour touched the ceiling above Lilli's head. Her spirits quickly lifted.

*Think only happy thoughts, dear Lilli.*

This was the sign she had been waiting for. Everything would be fine. Lilli was certain of it.

# CHAPTER THIRTEEN

A QUICK THUMP AT THE STILLROOM DOOR STOPPED LILLI in her tracks.

"What was that?" she asked, looking quickly in Alisz's direction. Surely Frau Hafner's husband was not expecting the remedy so soon. Alisz had not even had time to gather the herbs together, let alone create a salve. When another thump sounded immediately afterward, Alisz motioned for Lilli to remain quiet as she hurried toward the door. No one ever came to the stillroom door unless Alisz had invited them to do so. It was one of her rules. But Alisz was not expecting anyone this morning.

"Who is it?" Alisz asked, her hand pressed to the door. There came a faint rustling from the other side. A strange noise followed.

"I asked who it is," Alisz repeated—louder this time in case her voice could not be heard through the thick wooden door.

Still no answer came.

"No, Alisz!" whispered Lilli as Alisz slowly unlatched the door. It could be anyone outside, even someone meaning her harm. Vater was not the only one in Württemberg who disapproved of the use of certain plants and herbs. It had not been so many years since the witch trials. Lilli had only to look at Vater to know that the old beliefs were still very much alive.

Lilli looked on as Alisz opened the door far enough to see who it was. Why did Alisz not heed her warning? Alisz relaxed then and opened the door further, stepping aside so that Lilli could see who it was. A girl who looked to be Lilli's own age shifted her weight from one foot to the other, her arms folded awkwardly in front of her. She was but a wisp of a girl, but even a wisp of a girl could give one reason to fear, especially when they showed up without warning or invitation. Immediately, Lilli mistrusted her. Perhaps the girl's thin, narrow face and eyes that were too closely set made her wary. Or it could have been the peculiar feeling that plummeted through her when Lilli first saw the girl standing outside the door. Alisz always told her to pay close attention to the whispers that stirred inside her heart. They were difficult to ignore.

"What is it you want, child?" Alisz asked. Hearing the compassion in her voice made Lilli wince. Alisz was altogether too trusting. Even Mutter had said so.

Pushing a string of brown hair out of her face, the girl quickly hooked it behind her ear. She pushed her shoulders back.

"I am looking for the one they call Alisz. My bruder is fevering. Mutter has nothing to give him, nothing to use but cold cloths for his forehead. Someone said to come here, that Alisz would help him."

"Who said to come here?" Lilli asked, boldly moving forward. She must stop Alisz before she allowed this stranger to step foot inside her stillroom. The girl could be making this up for all they knew. She could have been sent here to spy. Alisz needed to be careful. There was much at stake should the wrong one discover what she did in the stillroom.

"Frau Eberhart, the butcher's wife," the girl replied through trembling lips. Lilli had been in the stillroom the day the butcher's wife came to Alisz begging for her help. Her eyes had been red from the tears that had spilled down across her cheeks.

"I do not wish to see another sunset if I am to go though life without a child," she had said. "Please tell me there is hope, that you have something that can help." Alisz had drawn an arm around Frau Eberhart's shoulder as she welcomed her inside. She sent Frau Eberhart away that day with some special herbs and a flicker of hope in her eyes. The last time Mutter and Lilli were in the village, they saw Frau Eberhart merrily singing. Her face was speckled with joy. Lilli did not have to wonder why. Her swollen belly told a story of its own.

"What did Frau Eberhart tell you?" asked Lilli, wondering how much of what this girl was about to say would be true.

"She said to come here and ask for Alisz. She said Alisz could help, that she can perform miracles. She said Alisz is kind and wise, with enough mercy to fill an entire ocean."

*Could* is a far cry from *would*, Lilli wanted to say. What made this girl so sure that Alisz would help her bruder—because the butcher's wife said so? Alisz did not even know them.

"Please help us," begged the girl, peering up at Alisz with yearning eyes. "He is burning up. Mutter is afraid he might die. Then what will we do? We are to leave for the New World soon. We cannot go without Jakob." Her words were filled with desperation. Her bottom lip continued to quiver. Tears would soon follow. Still, Lilli worried it could all be an act, to gain Alisz's trust.

"Come inside," said Alisz, motioning for the girl to enter the stillroom. "I have something that should help."

Lilli gazed at Alisz in disbelief. "But Alisz…," she cautioned once more.

"The willow bark, Lilli." Alisz spoke quietly but firmly. "Please take it from the shelf. We are here to help."

A wide smile stretched across the young girl's face. She quickly wiped her eyes with the palms of her hands. Staring at the jar of willow bark, Lilli refused to step out from behind the shelves. Alisz should not have invited this girl inside. It was simply too dangerous. The stillroom was secret, not meant for everyone to see. It was one of the very first lessons Alisz taught her all those years ago. They knew nothing about this girl—nothing.

With a quick eye, the girl looked all around the room. She drank in the sight of the plants dangling from the rafters, the jars filled with dried roots and herbs, the book with all of Alisz's remedies, missing not even the small bit of parched chamomile that had fallen to the floor. She saw it all.

"Lilli, please...someone is in need," said Alisz, forcing a polite smile. Lilli sighed. It was no good to argue with Alisz when she had her mind made up. She took the jar of willow bark off the shelf and placed it on the work table.

"What is your name, child?" Alisz asked. The girl shifted her eyes when Alisz spoke, casting them toward the floor.

"I am Hilda, Hilda Baumann." Her voice wobbled as if she had swallowed a bee. Lilli removed the top from the jar of willow bark. Many people from the village came for Alisz's remedies. It was what she did, who she was. Lilli could not imagine it being otherwise. If only Alisz would be more careful about who she allowed into her stillroom. It did not take much for someone to cry *witch*—if the wrong person ever found out.

"You live not far from here, then," said Alisz, nodding. The look she sent Lilli indicated that she thought this bit of news meant the girl could be trusted. Baumann—Lilli was familiar with the name as well, but that alone did not make this stranger trustworthy. The bag now filled with willow bark, Lilli pulled the string tight. With reluctance, she handed it to the girl.

"Only use a little at a time," said Alisz, indicating the amount with her fingers. "Give it a good boil, not too long, though. When it has cooled, have your bruder sip it until it is all gone. He will not like the taste, but it will bring down his fever."

The girl hesitated before reaching out to take it. "I...I have no money," she said. "Vater does not even have enough for our full passage to the New World. We will have to work to pay what remains once we arrive."

"Do not worry. Give this to your bruder." Alisz pressed the bag into Hilda's hands and squeezed tight. Hilda cried out thank you several times, and why not? She'd managed to take advantage of Alisz's good nature. Who was to say what would happen now, who she would go to, who she would tell?

"You should have sent her away empty-handed," said Lilli as soon as the door closed.

"Sometimes we need to have faith in others."

"Faith in the wrong person can be dangerous," said Lilli. Did Alisz not see the peril in this? These *others* Alisz spoke of were the very ones Lilli feared.

"Oh, worry, worry, worry, Lilli Eickle," said Alisz lightheartedly, turning back to her work. "You have the weight of the world on your shoulders."

"But Alisz," said Lilli shaking her head. She could not believe that Alisz had not thought of this. "What if Hilda is the fox?"

# CHAPTER FOURTEEN

SLEEP DID NOT SOME EASILY FOR LILLI THAT NIGHT. SHE thought about the girl, Hilda, and wondered if Alisz had not made a grave mistake by inviting her inside. What if Hilda told the wrong person about the plants she saw dangling from the rafters of the stillroom? Would Alisz be accused of witchcraft and put to trial the same way her oma had been? And did that mean that Lilli was also in danger?

Worry filled Lilli's mind as she drifted into the darkness of sleep. Soon she found herself in the flax field with Mutter beside her. Suddenly, there came a strange sound from overhead as a flock of birds passed quickly by. Black as night, their wing feathers fanned the air. Their cries spilled down like summer hailstones. Wings fluttered to a standstill as one by one the birds stopped to roost on the branches of the dead tree overlooking the flax field. Lilli turned her face toward the sky, and felt the breeze skim down across her cheeks. Landing, the birds formed an unusual pattern among the branches as hundreds of scaly feet gripped fast to the tree limbs. Lilli stood quietly watching, gazing toward the blue, blue sky. It was late summer.

*Chik chah...chik chah*, the birds chorused from the tree branches. They sounded angry. The clouds were thin, wispy, stretched out like dandelion fluff in a gentle breeze, not even strong enough to hold the cries of these noisy birds. Mutter called out to Lilli, drawing her attention away from the birds' noisy chatter.

"You must find Friedrich before he gets himself into mischief again," she said, gathering a bundle of flax in her arms.

"I am sure Friedrich is fine." It was too nice a day to waste time looking for her wayward bruder. Besides, there was work to be done.

"Lilli, please—hurry along, before Vater finds out he is gone," said Mutter sternly.

Friedrich could blend into his surroundings like a wood snipe settling into its nest, but she would find him, search him out wherever he was hiding. The birds roosting on the dead tree suddenly took to the sky, crying and cackling, taking their *chik chahs* with them. Lilli saw movement by the dead tree. Friedrich was climbing its branches. She marched toward the edge of the field, annoyed that Friedrich had allowed himself to be drawn away by the sound of some silly blackbirds.

"Come down out of that tree. You will fall to your death and then Mutter will be sad," she said.

"But I want to fly like a bird, Lilli."

"Friedrich!" Lilli made her voice as harsh as she dared without sounding like Vater. She did not wish to frighten him out of the tree. Should he slip and fall, she would be to blame.

Slowly, Friedrich backed down out of the tree, choosing his footing with care.

"We should pick a cornflower for Mutter before we head back. I found some the other day," said Lilli. "Blue is her favourite colour."

"Do you pick lavender when you visit with Alisz?" The question startled her. How much did Friedrich know about her days spent with Alisz?

"Why do you ask?" Turning her back to Friedrich, she swallowed the lump in her throat.

"I smell it in your hair sometimes. It smells nice." But of course, Friedrich did not know a thing about Alisz's herbs. She was worried for nothing. Tousling Friedrich's hair playfully, Lilli smiled.

"Hurry along, Friedrich. You walk much too slowly. A turtle could pass you without trying," she said, taking hold of his hand. Their laughter filled the air as they hurried toward the cornflowers. The birds appeared in the sky again, a large number of them, cawing as they passed overhead.

"It is a bad omen," said Friedrich, looking up at the birds.

"Do not talk so silly," Lilli told him. "They are just birds, Friedrich, flying through the sky. It is what birds do. Besides, bad omens do not exist. Alisz has even said so."

"But Vater says—"

"Forget Vater. He is set in his ways and too superstitious to stop himself from saying stupid things."

Friedrich's eyes grew wide. His mouth dropped open. Lilli did not know why she'd said those things to him. He would surely tell Vater and she would be punished for speaking with such disrespect. Still, she did not care. So many times she was forced to remain silent when Vater voiced his old-fashioned ideas. Her heart felt suddenly brave and strong. *The truth is not always pleasant, but it is the truth nonetheless and cannot go unspoken forever,* she thought. Vater was too superstitious for his own good.

"Here, let us pick a cornflower," said Lilli. Distracting Friedrich was not difficult, for he jumped around like a flea in a haystack most of the time.

"I will pick a large bunch for Mutter," said Friedrich as his plump hands reached out.

"No!" said Lilli, sharply. "We must respect Mother Earth. One stem is enough. If you pick them all, there will be none left for another time."

Reaching forward to pluck a cornflower, Lilli silently gave thanks to Mother Earth the way Alisz always did before taking any plants.

"Lilli!" cried Friedrich in horror, "Your hand! What is wrong with your hand?"

Lilli stared down at the place where her hand should have been. Blood and sinew, jagged bits of flesh dangled at the end of her arm. Her heart jumped into her throat. Shaking her hand, she willed it to come back into shape with fingers and a thumb. She screamed, but the sound dissolved into the wind. Blood splattered on the ground, bright red droplets dotted the green blades of grass near Lilly's feet. Above them, the blackbirds continued to circle, their cries piercing the air. Up and down they soared, moving in unison. Feathers fell earthward, showering Lilli with shadow. A chilling scream echoed across the landscape. The wind cut across the flax field, whipping up from out of nowhere, filling Lilli's lungs, tossing her screams away like falling leaves. Shaking, crying, she fell to her knees.

"It is a bad omen. It is a bad omen. It is a bad omen." The words kept repeating. They were Friedrich's. She ordered him to stop chanting. He ran off, his legs carrying him swiftly across the flax field toward Mutter. Lilli watched in disbelief as Friedrich opened his arms out wide and was lifted up into the air. A blackbird— Friedrich had become one of them.

Again, Lilli screamed.

In the background a voice was calling to her in the wind, so far in the distance it was little more than a whisper. Slowly, the sound grew in strength. Lilli stopped screaming long enough to listen. Her body heaved silently, worn and tired. The voice was now audible, clear as a crystalline lake.

Waking with a start, Lilli held fast to her fear as she suppressed the need to cry out. Moonlight found her, soothing her with its soft light. A whisper drifted her way in the dark. *"Your life will be torn apart. Separation is coming."*

Lilli knew then it was the dream that woke her, and the voice in the dream belonged to Alisz.

# CHAPTER FIFTEEN

"**L**AND GRANTS ARE BEING OFFERED FOR THOSE WILLING to settle in the New World," said Vater the next day as they sat down to their evening meal.

"I have heard that many are going," said Mutter, pouring some milk from the pitcher. The soup bubbled rapidly over the open hearth. Dipping up a steaming bowlful, Lilli set it on the table in front of Vater. She continued to dish out the meal, filling a bowl for Friedrich then Mutter, wondering about Vater's sudden interest in the New World. Was someone they knew going? It was no secret that ships had left Rotterdam last year and some were preparing to set sail this spring. It seemed there was little else anyone in the village talked about these days. Filling a bowl for herself, Lilli took her place at the table. They joined hands and bowed their heads, while Vater said the blessing over the food. He quickly opened his eyes and continued talking.

"Fifty acres for a family and ten for each dependant—I have been making inquiries." Vater blew into his soup, making snake-like patterns with his spoon before tasting it. He dipped some freshly baked bread into the broth and ate it hungrily. Lilli waited to hear what more he had to say, his reason for bringing the matter up in the first place. Reaching into his shirt pocket, he pulled out a paper and unfolded it. Smoothing out the creases, he passed it over to Mutter. Lilli glanced over Mutter's shoulder but could not see any of the words.

"John Dick—an agent for the British—he sets everything up. We could be on a ship as early as July," he said, stopping to look at Mutter. Lilli momentarily froze. July was only two months away. Surely Vater was not seriously thinking about them leaving Württemberg.

"July?" said Mutter, as if she had not heard him correctly. Vater nodded as pleasure travelled across his face. "And where will the money for this journey come from? A trip across the Atlantic will cost money—money we do not have."

Lilli felt a quick pulse of hope. Mutter was right. They were not rich by any means. There was no possible way they could afford such a trip. Vater was dreaming. He had been lured by some foolish promise made to him by someone he did not even know.

"I have been saving," said Vater. His eyes begged Mutter to understand how important this was to him.

"Saving...You have been saving?"

"Yes, saving," answered Vater eagerly.

"Without telling me, you have been saving?" Mutter's words seemed to come out in quiet protest, but would Vater even recognize her displeasure?

"Yes—for some time now. For many months I have been thinking and planning," said Vater, tapping his temple lightly. "This I did not think up overnight, Marta. It has been playing on my mind for a very long time. The well-being of this family is what matters most. This decision of mine is a good one, one that will benefit us all."

A multitude of possibilities danced in Vater's eyes as he sat at the table—his dreams of a new life, of owning land. What promises had this John Dick made to him, this man, this agent he knew nothing about? *Promises are no different than spider webs: pretty to look at but too fragile to grasp hold of,* Lilli wanted to cry out. Anyone could spurt off promises, scatter them around like seeds in a gale-force wind, and people would hurry to try and grab them.

"But still, you could not possibly have saved enough money for such a voyage. I have heard it is costly," said Mutter, putting her spoon to her lips. She refused to look up from her meal.

"We have possessions that can be sold. We cannot take everything with us."

Sell their possessions? Vater could not be serious. This had to be a joke, a cruel, ugly joke. They could not pick up and leave everything behind. Why, the thought was totally absurd. Lilli quickly looked toward Mutter. Mutter would put a stop to this. She had to.

"It appears you have thought of everything, Karl," she said softly. She dipped her spoon into the hot broth again. Her face gave no indication as to what her true feelings were.

"There is much to consider," said Vater. "A move such as this will be a big undertaking for this family. Yet as far as I can see, the advantages far outweigh any shortcomings there might be. Many have gone before us. We do not want to miss out on such an opportunity."

"But the Count," said Lilli. Surely the Count would not release them from their service to him.

"It is not for you to worry about these matters, Lilli. I will take care of this family. You need not question my abilities."

The voyage across the sea was brutal; everyone knew that— weeks and months without setting foot on dry land. There were stories of people who did not live to make the crossing. What could Vater be thinking?

The soup made a loud sound as Vater drew it through his lips. Lilli waited for Mutter to try and reason with him, to explain how dangerous such a voyage would be. When she failed to speak up, Lilli knew she must do something.

"But Vater," she said, earnestly setting her spoon down. She needed to choose her words with care. Vater would not tolerate any insolence from her. But surely, if he knew they were all against such a move, he would change his mind. "Württemberg is our home. It is where we belong."

"And we will make a new home on the other side of the world," said Vater, nodding as he spoke.

"But Vater—" Mutter sent Lilli a silent warning, but it was too late. The table rattled beneath the thump of Vater's clenched fist. Lilli jumped, nearly splattering her soup.

"I make the decisions for this family, Lilli. *I* decide what is best. And I will not have my judgement questioned. You are only a girl— a girl who has no say in these matters." His voice was growing in volume. Lilli dared not say another word.

"And what do the British want in return?" asked Mutter, inter-rupting his anger. With a face stroked with fury, his gaze rested momentarily on Lilli as if he were in a trance. She writhed beneath his stare, fearing what he might do. But then, Mutter reached out and touched his arm, breaking the spell. Blinking, he dipped his spoon into his soup again and resumed eating.

"The British—what would they want from us?" Mutter repeated. Lilli desperately needed to know what was going through her mind. The tone in Mutter's voice told her very little. Waiting for some expression to cross her face, Lilli saw only a blank stare. Surely, Mutter would not go along with this idea of Vater's. It made no sense for them to leave everything behind to start another life in a land they knew nothing about. And there was so much she still had to learn from Alisz. It would take many years of teaching. Alisz had said so herself. Lilli was a healer. It was something she was born to do. How could she continue her work with plants and herbs without Alisz?

"We would receive provisions for an entire year, tools for working the land, and material for building a home. It would give us a fresh start. Think of it, Marta. Our own land. To do with what we wish. Eickle land to have and to hold. It is what we have dreamed of."

Someone must have read what was on the paper to Vater. He was barely able to read, yet he recited the terms off as if he was well acquainted.

"*You*...it is what *you* have dreamed of," said Mutter, taking in a deep breath. "Now, I have asked several times—what do the British want in return?"

"We will work for them, clearing land, raising buildings—whatever is needed in this new land. They want good, strong Protestants to settle in the New World. There is much to be done." Vater wiped his mouth against his sleeve.

"But of course. There is always something. They are not doing this out of the goodness of their hearts," said Mutter, looking down into her bowl. "How long would we be required to work for the British, then?"

"The land is rich in Nova Scotia. John Dick has said that—"

"How long?" repeated Mutter firmly. "How long would we work for the British?"

Vater set his spoon down and carefully folded his hands, resting his elbows firmly on the table. His resolve was unwavering. Mutter could ask all the questions she wished and it would make no difference. His mind was already made up. It was plain to see.

"No one can expect a parcel of land without giving something in return, Marta. We may not have much to offer, but we have good, strong backs. It is a fair trade. That is all you need to know."

The tension in the air was thick as week-old curd. Vater was not willing to consider how they would feel about such a move, even though it involved them all.

"There is a boat leaving in July," he continued, reaching for his spoon again. "We will be on it."

July—that was impossible. Lilli jumped up from the table. She was through being patient. "Lilli, no!" Mutter scolded, grabbing her by the arm. But it was too late.

"We cannot leave here, Vater. This is our home. This is where we belong. This New World you speak of, this phantom land, we know nothing about it. How can you even consider such a move?"

"Lilli, sit down and eat your meal," barked Vater, thrusting his fist onto the table with the force of a thunderstorm. "I alone make the decisions for this family."

Desperation fanned the air in Lilli's lungs. Someone had to change Vater's mind. She turned toward Mutter. Perhaps she could persuade him. If only she would speak up.

"Mutter, please. You must tell Vater you do not want to leave. Tell him."

Searching Mutter's face for reassurance, Lilli waited for her to speak up and tell him that they would not be leaving Württemberg—not now, not ever.

"Lilli, this is not a matter for you to decide upon," said Mutter, hushing her as if she had no right to object.

Friedrich jumped up from the table just then and began dancing around.

"We are going to sail across the sea," he chimed, his arms whirling and flapping like a bird about to take flight.

"Friedrich, you should quiet down," said Vater. His words to Friedrich were no louder than the bleating of a lamb. He knew Lilli was upset, yet he was pleased to see that Friedrich was excited about moving to the New World.

"We are going to live in a bright, shiny new world," cried Friedrich, now hopping in a circle from one foot to the other. A smile settled on Vater's lips as he watched Friedrich dancing. It was more than Lilli could stand.

Reeling toward Friedrich, Lilli cried, "What do you know?" as Friedrich continued his dance.

"Friedrich, please. Eat your meal and stop parading about," said Mutter, her voice bending in anger. Stopped in his tracks by Mutter's scolding, Friedrich slid back onto his seat.

An awkward silence settled over them. The air made no apologies. Words and sound no longer existed. Lilli wanted to speak, but the thoughts in her head could not find a way to her tongue. At last, Friedrich squirmed in his seat, breaking the stillness. Lilli gathered her bowl from the table, unable to eat. Her hand brushed against one of the candles on the table and it toppled over. She quickly righted it, but not before some wax spilled from the candle, hardening into a smooth, round orb. "Lilli, please fetch something to clean this," Mutter ordered.

"Mutter," Lilli pleaded softly as she handed her a rag. "We cannot leave Württemberg. This is our home. It is where we belong." How could she become a healer in this New World without Alisz to teach her?

"Still your tongue, my child. There is nothing I can do," whispered Mutter.

But there had to be something Mutter could do—something Lilli could do. She stared down at the candle wax on the table, wishing an answer would reveal itself to her.

### NEW GERMANY, NOVA SCOTIA, 2019

"That's it!" said Lilly, pointing to the computer screen. "It's what I saw in my dream. Only it wasn't a painting, it was real. I knew it! Walpurgisnacht really is a thing." She had described her dream to Alice and how clearly she'd heard the word *Walpurgisnacht* spoken. But to see it and know it was actually real filled Lilly with sense of relief. Her mind hadn't just made it up.

"I've never heard of this Walpurgisnacht, but I do like the way it sounds," said Alice, looking at the fiery images on the screen—the orange and yellow flames dancing into the night. "It looks rather frightening." The paintings and pictures were just like the scenes from Lilly's dream, with shadowy figures surrounding a large bonfire.

"I've never heard of it either, until last night." Lilly looked up at Alice. She didn't blame Alice for not believing her right away; a part of her wasn't sure what to think either. Now she had found the proof. But how could a word she'd never heard before come to her in a dream? It was all very confusing. Lilly continued to scan the screen.

"It's also called Walpurgis Night, the night when witches meet on the highest mountain in Germany, known as the Brocken mountain. So that means *Walpurgisnacht* is a German word."

"Are you saying we were witches in a past life, you and me?" said Alice, smiling.

"You promised you wouldn't make fun," said Lilly, searching the site for more information.

"I wasn't making fun. In fact, I quite like that idea of being a witch," said Alice. Smiling, she moved closer to the screen. "It says to ward off the witches' evil, people burnt bonfires, beat the ground with sticks and broomsticks, cracked whips, rang bells, and shouted. They thought noise was the best way to keep evil away."

"There was lots of noise in my dream," said Lilly. "According to ancient legend, Walpurgisnacht is the last chance for witches to stir up trouble before the land reawakens in spring. It says here's it's April 30th. That's next week!" Lilly looked up at Alice. "What if my dreams have something to do with Walpurgisnacht?"

"I suppose it could." Alice sounded doubtful. "It says they still celebrate it today, but it's to welcome spring, not chase away evil. Well, it's good to know things have evolved a certain amount," said Alice.

Lilly pointed to the screen again, "Some believe that on Walpurgis Night the barrier between our world and the supernatural can easily be crossed. It's when the veil between the worlds is thinnest." She looked up at Alice. "I wonder what that means?"

The more Lilly read, the more she was convinced that somehow this Walpurgisnacht held the key.

# CHAPTER SIXTEEN

THE FULL MOON CAST SHADOWS ON THE EARTH, dipping into the cradle hills, sliding out across the knolls and rocks. Lilli looked toward the gentle sound of flapping wings overhead as an owl glided quietly past. Stopping in her tracks, Alisz grabbed hold of Lilli's hand. "What is that sound?" she whispered.

In the stillness that followed, Lilli heard only the soft, filtered voice of the wind stirring through the leaves, a whisper of the past, present, and what was to be.

"I did not hear a thing," Alisz replied, twisting the handle of her basket. Lilli needed to tell her about Vater's plan for them sail to the New World. It was all she had been thinking about since Vater first thrust this plan of his upon them last week. It clung to her like a wet shawl, and no matter how hard she tried to shed it, to think those happy thoughts Alisz insisted upon, she could not.

"Alisz, there is something I need to tell you—"

"Shh," cautioned Alisz. "There it is again. Listen."

From a nearby tree, the owl sent a quiet warning into the night.

"Someone is coming," gasped Lilli.

"Hurry...to the woods," whispered Alisz as the soft thumping in the distance gradually came nearer and louder. The ground beneath them began to rumble as two horses and their riders approached in the moonlight, their silhouettes passing through the dark like phantoms out on a ghostly ride. Alisz murmured a soft plea to the Night Goddess, asking her for protection. "Keep going," she pleaded quietly, "keep going."

Lilli drew in a deep breath as the horses quickly came to a halt.

"What is this?" a deep voice thundered into the night, an echo so loud that it swallowed the full moon in one gulp.

As she peeked out through the trees, Lilli saw a shadowy rider reach down and snatch something off the ground.

"My basket!" gasped Lilli, bringing her hand to her mouth. In her hurry to escape, she had left it behind on the ground. If they were found out, it would be her fault. Alisz made a soft shushing sound and held her tight.

"Do not touch it," came another voice. "It could be the work of witches!" The garden became covered in darkness as the clouds above them sifted, snuffing out the light.

Lilli trembled. She steadied herself against Alisz. The strip of woods was narrow, and beyond that was a wheat field. If the riders searched the woods, there would be no place to go, nowhere to escape to without being seen. The horses moved restlessly back and forth as they snorted and heaved.

"Witch! Come out, witch! Come show yourself if you are near!"

An empty laugh echoed far into the night, disappearing into the mouth of the wind.

"Witch!" The word quivered like a long-held secret finally released into the world.

"Where is your witch? There is no one here."

"Perhaps she made herself disappear."

Hard laughter tumbled across the expanse like an angry fist punching into the air. The moon peeked out from behind a tattered veil as the silhouettes became visible again. One of the riders let out a shrill whistle and the horses began to knead the earth with their feet, uprooting Alisz's plants as they stepped back and forth across the garden. A strong arm of disbelief drew Lilli near. The riders were not going to leave until every last plant had been destroyed. She longed to scream out at them, demand they leave, but there was nothing she could do. Helpless to make them stop, Lilli pushed her face against the bark of a white pine tree and waited.

Time stretched onward, gradually pulling each minute apart like dandelion cotton until Lilli could not be certain how much time had lapsed.

"They are leaving," Alisz finally whispered as Lilli looked out from behind the pine tree.

When the rumble of hoof beats dissolved into the darkness of night, Alisz hurried toward what was left of the garden. Lilli followed close behind, stopping the moment she felt the soft ground beneath her feet. The pungent scent of fresh-turned earth was all around.

"Your plants, Alisz!" she cried out as a thousand drums beat in her ears. Hurriedly, she stepped toward her basket.

"Do not fret, Lilli. Gardens can be replaced," said Alisz. She took the trampled basket from Lilli and attempted to straighten the handle.

"But Alisz, all your work…your healing plants! They will be hard to replace."

"I have suffered other setbacks, some far greater than this. It is the price we sometimes pay when we follow our true nature. You must remember that for everything we experience in life there is a reason. Have faith and know the time is coming when people will no longer fear the things they do not understand. And when that time comes, there will be no need for secret gardens."

"But Alisz, this is not fair. How can they be so stupid?" A breeze caused the leaves on the trees to quake. Lilli struggled to hold back tears. She did not want Alisz to see how weak she was.

"Fear will govern the heart if we let it, Lilli. It causes people to act in appalling ways. You must not worry, though. The garden will come back to life. Everything does in its own time." Alisz drew in a deep, cleansing breath.

Just then, hope poured through Lilli's veins. "You mean there is some incantation?" she said. But of course, Alisz would know what to do. She always did.

"No. I'm afraid nothing so mystical. I have seeds in my still-room. We shall simply start over again, in another location. I shall have to find a better hiding place is all."

"But that will take many months."

"Then we will require patience," said Alisz calmly as she began the journey back home. As she always did, Alisz sounded optimistic about the future. Lilli had rarely, if ever, heard her complain. But to lose her garden...it was a big loss. These plants did not grow readily in the wild. They were the ones that some people called witches' plants, the very reason she had to grow them in secret.

"We should go," said Alisz, turning away from her trampled garden. Lilli's feet refused to propel her forward, not until she had spoken the truth out loud. She had to tell Alisz about Vater's plan to leave. She would not be here to see the garden grow.

"Come along, it is getting late." Alisz motioned for Lilli to catch up.

"But Alisz, you do not understand. There will be no time for me." Running to catch up to Alisz, she blurted out in desperation, "Vater wants to leave for the New World. He has saved money."

Alisz stopped abruptly in her tracks and turned toward Lilli.

"I see," she said.

"The next ship leaves in July. Vater says we will be on it."

"Many people are making plans to go to this New World. I hear them talking in the village. They are excited about the prospect of owning land," said Alisz softly.

"Land!" snorted Lilli, shaking her head.

"The promise of land is nothing to be ignored. I have seen men lured by far less."

"Then they are stupid. No one knows what this New World is like, the dangers that might be there."

"There will be many new opportunities awaiting those who go. To arrive in a new land…" Alisz paused and looked back at Lilli. She gave a faint smile. "It will help if you think positive thoughts."

Positive thoughts? New opportunities? What was Alisz saying? Did she not realize the thought of starting a new life on the other side of the world was making her ill? There was nothing positive about this idea of Vater's, not a thing. Alisz was mistaken.

"What does your mother think about all this?" Alisz asked, clearing her throat.

"I am not sure. She has not said. She will not go against Vater. It is not her place to do so. He is selfish and thinks only of him-self." Whenever Lilli tried to talk about their leaving, Mutter would change the subject, but that did not keep the sadness from rising to the surface of her face whenever she thought no one was looking.

This was like a horrible dream that Lilli could not wake from. She could not imagine the wide-open sea separating her from her home, from all she knew and loved, from Alisz. And as she looked up at Alisz with hope-filled eyes, she suddenly had an idea.

# CHAPTER SEVENTEEN

**T**HE OWL CALLED SOFTLY TO THEM FROM THE DISTANCE. "You could come to the New World too, Alisz," said Lilli, grasping hold of Alisz's hands. Alisz was like family. There was no reason for her to stay behind. If they did have to leave Württemberg, she might be able to bear it if Alisz was by her side. They could continue their work together, become healers in the New World. Surely there were sick there and babies to be born.

"Lilli, please…"

"No, Alisz, listen to me. The British would be happy to have you," continued Lilli, excitedly. "You are healthy and strong. You could work off your fare. Many people are doing just that."

"Lilli—" Alisz spoke more forcefully this time.

"You could bring your herbs to the New World and help people there. There is sure to be sickness in this new land. And there is still so much you can teach me. There will be babies to bring into the world. People will need your help," she continued, presenting the idea to Alisz like a treasured gift. The more she spoke, the more sense it made.

Moonbeams cascaded down upon them and a sad smile crossed Alisz's face.

"My dear Lilli, there are already people in the New World, people who have lived there since long before the British ever thought of coming. I have heard they can make medicines even better than our own. Their knowledge goes back many centuries.

Lilli shook her head. "Why are you telling me this?"

"You could learn from them about the plants that grow there." Alisz paused. "That is, if you are willing to stay receptive. And besides, have you forgotten about all those who come to me for help here? There is no one else for miles around. Who will treat them? And there is my garden to replant. I have taught you much of what I know. You will take this knowledge with you to this new land. Your future has already been set in motion. It is the way things must be, dear Lilli. We do not always have a say in the path fate has shaped for us."

Lilli was tired of hearing about what must be, and tired of accepting that she was at the mercy of a world that did not care. Surely there was some way to stop Vater from uprooting the family.

"Promise me you'll think about it," Lilli said in desperation.

Alisz shook her head. "I shall keep my feet on dry land, thank you. I could not bear to be tossed about on the sea. I know it sounds silly, but most fears are. It does not make them any less real. If I panicked on my way across the water, what would I do? I would have no place to go. No way to escape."

"You have said many times that we should face our fears. I will help you!" Lilli looked eagerly at Alisz. "You are not an old man fishing on the sea, Alisz. You are a wise woman—a healer and midwife."

"Dear Lilli, this is something you cannot understand, for I do not understand it myself. But I ask that you please respect my fears."

"I will stay here with you, then." Lilli was thirteen, after all; soon old enough to make her own decisions. The answer was simple. She could stay in Württemberg with Alisz and become the healer and midwife she was meant to be. Mutter and Vater would still have Friedrich. It made perfect sense.

"My dear Lilli. I could not keep you from your family. It would not be right. We do the things that life requires of us. Often they are not the easiest. Change does not come about painlessly. But in time you will come to think of this new place as home. I promise."

"But I do not want to leave. *This* is home, not some new land on the other side of the world. How can this be something that must happen? We do not even know what is waiting for us there. Vater should just go by himself. It was his idea. He could take Friedrich. Mutter and I could stay here." She had heard Mutter's muffled cries in the night. In the morning her eyes were red and swollen.

"We all do things we do not want to, Lilli," said Alisz. "You must remember, 'the path is not long, but the way is deep. You must not only walk there, you must be prepared to leap.'"

Why was Alisz using the words of Hildegard? "But it is not fair," Lilli cried out. Alisz was just being stubborn. Was her garden really that important to her, her fear of water so strong? Why would she choose to remain in Württemberg, hiding who she was, and what she did, for fear that the wrong person might find out, when there was a whole new world waiting for her, one that had not passed judgement?

Times were changing, as Alisz said, but not quickly enough for Lilli. The witch trials had happened many years ago, yet even now it took very little for someone to cry witch. People in Württemberg were still mumbling about Frau Ludwig and her baby, looking for more proof that the child was bewitched. Many women in Württemberg would not even look at the child, for fear of having a spell cast over them. Alisz would never be truly safe.

But then another idea struck Lilli. Perhaps there was a way for them to stay after all.

"Is there some charm in the book, something to make Vater stay?" said Lilli. The night wind murmured a soft song through the trees as she waited for Alisz's reply.

"I am sorry, Lilli, but there is no charm to keep a man in his homeland. Not one that I know of."

"But the book is filled with charms and incantations. You stopped my dreams; surely you can stop Vater. I would rather die than leave Württemberg. This is home to me."

"Stopping bad dreams is one thing, dear Lilli, but this…" Alisz shook her head slowly. "This is a family matter, and there is nothing I can do. There is a time and a season for everything in life. Things that come to pass happen for a reason. It is the way the world works. Right now you do not understand what that reason is, but I promise that one day you will. I am sorry, but for now, I cannot interfere. Even if I knew of something. I would not…"

"But Alisz—"

Alisz touched Lilli's cheek. "Life does not always treat us the way we would like. I know this better than most. But to interfere with the natural order of things could prove catastrophic," said Alisz, shaking her head.

Tears pushed against the back of Lilli's eyes. She did not want to hear Alisz talk about things happening for a reason. She wanted Alisz to tell her that everything would be fine, that she could change Vater's mind about leaving. But within the quiet folds of darkness, the night held them captive. There were no more words to say, or hopes to be had; no more promises to be made. What was to be would be.

"Look at that moon, Lilli," whispered Alisz, suddenly turning her face toward the sky. "The Goddess is smiling down at us."

"Alisz, no." Lilli was not interested in looking at the moon.

"Can you not feel its pull, its mighty power?" Alisz said.

The breeze refused to go unnoticed. It was cleansing and fresh, whipping Lilli's sadness out from under her and releasing it into the night air. She looked upward as if some force compelled her to do so. Tears blurred her vision, but she did not wipe them away. Stars filled the sky, splattered in clusters that produced the patterns Lilli had grown familiar with over the years. The moon was gigantic. Its magic drenched Lilli, showering her with silvery beams, grounding her to the earth by a strange mystical power.

"It is so strong," said Lilli, finally welcoming the night breeze against her face. She looked over at Alisz. Moonlight reflected off her face, picking out the copper tones in her cinnamon hair. Surely, Alisz was mistaken. There had to be some way to stop Vater.

"We must hurry along. Your mother will worry," said Alisz.

In the heavens directly above them, a star streaked earthward. Lilli quickly made a wish. There might be a reason for everything in life, just as Alisz said, but that did not mean they could not change things from time to time.

Moving through the quiet of the moonlit night, a spark of hope ignited inside her. Lilli knew then what she must do.

# CHAPTER EIGHTEEN

WÜRTTEMBERG, 1752

"**S**LOW DOWN," SAID LILLI, INCREASING HER STEPS. Why was Alisz in such a hurry? She usually took her time when they were out wandering in the woods, listening to the birds and paying close attention to the plants they saw along the way, sometimes even stopping to talk to them.

"Why will you not tell me where we are going?" she said. Alisz was carrying a basket covered with a piece of linen cloth, and she would not let Lilli see what was inside.

"Patience, dear Lilli; you need only follow for now."

"But you are being mysterious," said Lilli when she finally caught up.

Late last week, Alisz had spoken of a surprise she wanted to give Lilli the next time she came to the cottage. Lilli had been trying to imagine what that surprise might be. At least it had given her things to think about other than their leaving for the New World in July. It had been weeks since Vater first broke the news, and Lilli was desperately trying to come up with a way to carry out her plan to keep them from going. Time was quickly closing in. Already, it was June.

She knew what needed to be done, but she had yet to work out all the details. She had thought it through carefully, imagined a happy outcome in her mind's eye, with Vater laughing and telling her they were staying in Württemberg after all. If only she did not have to go behind Alisz's back to accomplish it.

They passed through several fields before entering a forested area where Lilli had never been before. The air was warm. The warbles of songbirds followed them through the woods. The trees formed a green canopy above them, shutting out much of the sunlight. The shade was welcomed.

Alisz looked over at Lilli. "Promise me you will never stop being inquisitive. It is a trait that will serve you well as you go through life," she said, smiling.

"Alisz," Lilli begged, finally stopping in her tracks. "It is not fair. What is this surprise? What do you have in your basket?"

"Bear with me. It is not far now, but it will be worth the walk. I promise."

"Did you find some horehound?" Lilli asked excitedly as she ran to catch up. "That's it, isn't it? You discovered some horehound on your travels." The ancient writings of the Hildegard von Bingen contained a promising cure Alisz was anxious to try. The recipe called for equal parts of dill, fennel, and horehound to be boiled in wine and strained through linen cloth. It was said to be an excellent cure for a persistent cough. But there was no horehound nearby. Alisz had been searching for a supply of the astringent herb since late last summer but so far had been unable to locate any. Until she had tested the cure herself, she would not write about it in her book.

"I am afraid to say that I am still searching for the elusive horehound. I expect it will show up one day when I least expect it." Alisz slowed her pace, stopping at a small clearing in the forest. The spot was sunny despite being surrounded by trees. "We are here," she said.

Lilli looked above her. It was as if the trees were opening their branches up to allow the sunshine in. She knew immediately why Alisz brought her here. It was a most beautiful location; breathtaking.

"I stumbled upon this place many years ago while I was out foraging for plants. I come here on occasion to be alone and to simply bask in the beauty. The earth is rich," said Alisz, picking up a handful of dirt.

"You're putting your secret garden here?"

"I have often thought about growing some herbs here, and now, with my garden gone, I would certainly have an excuse to begin. But I do not want to disturb the beauty of this place. I am sure I will find the perfect location in time, perhaps even better than the first."

"Why do you always do that?" asked Lilli.

"Do what?" Alisz gave her a puzzled look.

"You take something bad and turn it into a good thing."

"What choice do I have, Lilli? Besides, if you look closely enough, there is usually some good that can come from a tragedy. But you have to *want* to see that good. Lamenting over our losses only keeps us stuck in the past. I will not let a few lost plants keep me down. Now, please," said Alisz, kneeling, "sit. We are going to do a soul-friend ceremony."

"Soul-friend ceremony? What is that?" said Lilli, kneeling on the ground opposite Alisz.

"A ceremony that will join us together in friendship. I know you are sad to be leaving. This ceremony will seal the bond of our friendship forever. In this life and beyond," said Alisz. Removing the linen cloth from the basket, she spread it on the ground before them. She took the items from the basket. First she removed three candle holders and placed candles in them. After that came three goblets, two small and one large. She placed them all on the linen cloth while Lilli silently watched. Next she removed a flask from the basket and finally her tinderbox.

Taking the lid from the tinderbox, she struck the flint until a small shower of sparks formed a tiny ember onto the unspun flax. Gently blowing onto it, she coaxed it to life. Igniting a wooden splint, she used it to light the candles, and when she was through, she snuffed out the smouldering ember with the lid. Pouring some herbal tea from the flask into each of the smaller cups, she explained the steps to the ritual. The air was still. Sunshine danced upon them; the trees whispered a soft sonnet. And they began.

They each sipped from one of the smaller goblets and then, exchanging cups, took another drink. The remains were poured into the larger goblet—the unity chalice, Alisz explained.

"I am your friend," said Alisz as they began stating their friendship intentions.

"I am also *your* friend," replied Lilli.

"I am your teacher," said Alisz.

"I am your apprentice," replied Lilli.

"I am your guardian," stated Alisz.

"I am your comfort," replied Lilli. Once their friendship intentions were stated, they took turns drinking from the large unity chalice. At the end of the ceremony, Alisz gave Lilli a small gift wrapped in linen.

"Open it," she said, smiling. "This is all part of the ceremony."

"But Alisz, I have nothing for you," said Lilli, quickly unwrapping the linen.

Inside was a small pendant with an unusual stone in the centre.

"So many beautiful colours!" cried Lilli as sunbeams illuminated the many colours in the tiny stone.

"It is a rainbow moonstone, and is said to have special powers that allow the wearer to tap into past lives and memories. Legend has it that the stones are the frozen tears shed by the Moon Goddess after a lovers' quarrel. It belonged to Oma. She gave it to me days before she was accused of being a witch and taken away." The stone was wrapped in a thin piece of copper wire and attached to a leather string.

"But Alisz, I cannot—" It was far too generous a gift.

"Be still, dear soul-friend," said Alisz, smiling. "We are joined now in this life and beyond. This pendant represents just that. Take it with you to this new land you are going to."

As Lilli slipped the pendant over her head, she wondered if the rainbow moonstone would really join them together in this life, and whether it meant her plan to change Vater's mind about leaving would really work.

# CHAPTER NINETEEN

SWIFTLY, SILENTLY, LILLI DARTED THROUGH THE TREES
that surrounded Alisz's home. Clinging to the trunk of a linden
tree, she waited. It was Alisz's day to gather wild herbs from the
forest. She waited for Alisz to leave the house and then hastened
her way through Alisz's flower garden, slipping into the quiet of the
empty stillroom. The aroma of dried rosemary and sage met her
in the doorway. It fluttered about the room like a bird, filling her
with bitter longing. If she was not able to change Vater's mind, all
the things she loved so dearly would be lost. She could not imagine
never sitting by the hearth in the evening helping Mutter spin wool
or gathering herbs and roots with Alisz; never setting foot inside
the stillroom again; never becoming a healer.

She hurried to where Alisz kept her book. Alisz said otherwise,
but surely there was something within the covers, some way to
change Vater's mind about leaving, something Alisz did not know
about. The book held many secrets, some of which Lilli already knew,

and many of which she had not yet learned. If she could not find an incantation in the book, she would have to come up with one of her own. She had seen Alisz create new remedies on more than one occasion. It might not be so difficult to put together a charm. Positive—she must think only positive thoughts. She wrapped her fingers around the rainbow moonstone for courage.

Lilli paused, her hand resting on the book. A small voice deep inside nudged her. This was Alisz's most prized possession—the wisdom and knowledge of the women in her family, passed down over generations. Was it right to go through the book without permission? But she and Alisz were now soul-friends. They were meant to be together. Alisz was the wisest person she knew. Somehow Lilli would take that same wisdom and make it work for her. She would find a way to stay in Württemberg.

Lilli pulled in a breath before opening the book. Her cause was admirable, not meant to do any harm. There was so much to be gained if she succeeded in her quest. Besides, she had leafed through the book numerous times while in Alisz's company—was this really any different? If she could make Vater change his mind about leaving Württemberg, Alisz would thank her later. Alisz said she could not interfere; there was nothing she could do. It was not fair to have asked for her help. Lilli could see that now. Alisz was right: this was a family matter.

"I cannot meddle in something that should not concern me," Alisz had said. "If I could, Lilli, I most surely would. But my interference could bring about devastating results." Tears brimmed Alisz's eyes as she forced a smile, but Lilli had not been fooled. Alisz did not want them to go. The only ones who were happy about their leaving were Friedrich and Vater. What did they know? Vater's sights were set on owning land; Friedrich's, the adventure he imagined awaited him in a land on the other side of the world. Did they not care that with all of this there was certain to be risks, dangers of which they could not even imagine? If they boarded the ship, there were no guarantees they would all arrive safely.

"The countryside is so beautiful this time of year," Mutter had said last week as she looked out across the field, her sigh heavy.

"Can you not change Vater's mind?" Lilli had asked for the hundredth time.

Lilli now carefully turned the pages of Alisz's book so as not to damage the aged parchment. When she came to the place marked *Spells and Charms*, she stopped. The list was long, taking up several pages, the writing small—*Spells for lost love, Spells for happiness, Spells for good health.* Her hand trembled as her finger moved down the first page. Turning to the next one, she continued her search, stopping abruptly when she came to: *Spells for changing the mind of another.* That had to be it! Surely this was what she was looking for. Lilli read through the list, scanning the ingredients quickly.

> *To be placed in a small bag:*
> *A small amount of mugwort*
> *Four strands of couch grass*
> *Liquorice root*
> *Write the person's name in freshly turned earth, then add the earth to the bag.*
> *For best results, wait until the moon is full.*

The moon was now waning, little more than a thumbnail in the sky. She would have to wait for the right time. She would only have one chance, and there was no room for mistakes.

At the bottom of the list was a notation in dark letters.

*Caution: Care should be taken when doing this incantation, as it has been known to change someone's mind for the worse instead of the better.*

Worse instead of better? Lilli knew she need not worry. That would be impossible. There were only two choices—to go to the New World or to stay in Württemberg. Nothing could be worse than their leaving Württemberg.

She got right to work gathering the herbs she needed.

*Mugwort*—it was on the shelf next to the feverfew. She had to hurry. Removing the top from the jar, she quickly sprinkled a generous amount in her kerchief. If a little was good, a lot would be better. Vater was a stubborn man.

*Couch grass*—an abundant supply grew along the edges of their garden. It could be gathered any time. Mutter was forever complaining about its invasive nature.

*Liquorice*—there were various jars of roots to choose from, but liquorice was one she had seen Alisz use on more than one occasion. Quickly locating the right jar, she removed a small piece of liquorice root and placed it in the kerchief along with the mugwort.

Fumbling with the ends of the kerchief, she tied it up in a crude fashion. Just as she placed the stopper in the jar of liquorice root, the door behind her creaked. Lilli froze. Had Alisz returned already? What would she tell her? She could not look her in the eye and tell a lie. They were soul-friends. Alisz would see right through her.

Slipping the kerchief into her dress pocket, she spun around.

Hilda! Lilli could not believe her eyes. What was she doing here? And why was she sneaking around Alisz's house when Alisz was not at home? This only proved she was not to be trusted. She was indeed the fox from Alisz's dream, the one who would betray her, but Alisz would not listen.

"You!" Lilli shrieked. "What are you doing here, little spy?" Observing the way Hilda pulled her basket close, she added, "Have you come here to help yourself to Alisz's herbs?"

Hilda's bright blue eyes expanded. If she were smart, she would run away and never come back. She had no business being here in the first place, no business at all.

"I was not...I am not...," she stammered.

"You are not what, spying on Alisz? Then tell me, why are you here? You have no right coming into Alisz's house when she is not home." Lilli was determined to get to the bottom of this. Alisz might think that Hilda was harmless, but Lilli would prove otherwise. She would show her for the threat that she was.

"The door was open a crack," said Hilda, her voice trembling. "I heard someone inside." Tears wetted her eyes. "I saw no harm."

"So you thought you would walk right in? Who sent you?" If someone had sent her to spy, Lilli would find out who it was.

"It was Mutter. Mutter sent me to...to thank Alisz. My bruder is better. The willow bark—it worked. We will be able to make the trip across the Atlantic," she squeaked.

"Then what have you there?" demanded Lilli, glaring at the basket Hilda was carrying.

"Mutter sent it. She wanted me to give this to Alisz." Reaching beneath the cloth, she pulled out a small jar.

"Honey." The word caught in Lilli's throat as she gazed at the jar filled with the golden liquid. It was a generous gift. Alisz would be most grateful.

"Will you see that she gets it?"

Setting the jar on the table, Hilda hurried out the door.

Lilli should have called out to her, but could not bring herself to do so. She had been so sure Hilda was the fox from Alisz's dreams, positive that she was the one who would betray her.

As Lilli looked about the stillroom one last time to make sure nothing was out of place, an odd sensation pricked her heart. She felt for the bulk of herbs in her pocket. Alisz trusted her and she had taken advantage of that trust. *But it is for the best*, she silently cried. Once Vater changed his mind about this voyage to the New World she would confess her misdeed to Alisz. Reaching for the jar of honey, she placed the offering on the ground outside the stillroom for Alisz to find. Whispering a prayer for forgiveness, she closed the door.

# CHAPTER TWENTY

"**Y**OU WILL NEED CHAMOMILE AND DANDELION ROOT, peppermint leaves, raspberry leaf as well. There are so many things to remember," said Alisz, filling Lilli's arms with jars of dried herbs. "Some elderberry—infections are to be anticipated sooner or later; aches and pains as well. It is difficult to say what will be growing in this new land you are off to. I will pack plenty of seeds as well. In time, you may need to plant your own garden. Your work is important. Others will come to depend upon you. The work must be continued regardless of where you are. Remember that, Lilli. You are a born healer. I saw it in the stars the night you were born." Setting the jars out on the table, Alisz hurried to the shelves for more.

The apprehension in the air buzzed about the stillroom like a tormented bee. If only Alisz would slow down, perhaps they could talk. Lilli longed for some of Alisz's silly talk to lighten the mood. All morning she scuttled about the stillroom like a water beetle, her face marked in serious contemplation.

These past few weeks had been heartbreaking for Lilli, watching Vater sell off the remnants of their life in Württemberg. The livestock were to be sold tomorrow, all but the oxen that would take them, and what meagre belongings they had left, to the Rhine. Arrangements had been made for someone to buy the oxen and the wagon once they made it to the river. She had overheard Vater one evening telling Mutter. From there, they would travel down the river by raft to Rotterdam—or so was Vater's plan. But Lilli would not allow herself to worry about their belongings. Once Vater called the trip off, they could buy more supplies with the money he had saved for the voyage. Everything would be fine.

Tomorrow night she would perform the incantation. The moon was near full; the book said it was the best time. The waiting this past while had been excruciatingly difficult. She had been preparing herself for weeks: thinking and planning about the best time and place. Worry begged for her friendship, following her like a hungry fox, but she refused to offer any morsels. Each time, she pushed it away, using all the strength she could summon. At night she gave her prayers over to the Goddess, asking that the incantation work. Envisioning a positive outcome in her mind, sleep would eventually carry her away. She would get only one chance to change the course of her life.

Time was spinning at an uncontrollable speed, the stars aligning in a most unusual pattern in the night sky, and it filled Lilli with hope. She told Mutter, but she had only looked at Lilli and said, "You are dreaming, Lilli. The stars are the same as they have been for centuries."

Alisz's mind was also spinning too fast. Why would she not slow down? It was not like her to be so anxious.

"The crossing will be the most difficult. There is sure to be sickness on the ship, but I will make sure you are well prepared. Now, willow bark is most important. You know that, right, Lilli?" Lilli nodded. Willow bark would fight fever and was one of the simplest and best remedies she knew. Lilli glanced over at Alisz's herb book. It was filled with mystery and knowledge and more remedies than could be counted. Would she even remember what to do with the herbs once she arrived in the New World without the book to guide her? But no, there would be nothing to worry about, she reminded herself again. The incantation would take care of it all. It had to.

"But of course you know all that. You did not spend these past eight years with your head in the clouds. You were a willing student from the very start, so eager to learn. I knew you were the one who was to carry on the work. I made a good choice. You have not disappointed me."

"But I have not left yet," said Lilli, smiling. "Perhaps there is still time for fate to change its course."

"That may be so, but in the meantime you must prepare for what is before you now, Lilli. You cannot ignore the path you are on, no matter how you might wish for another. Hope is important, but so is keeping one's head about them," said Alisz, hurrying once again to the shelves.

"Alisz...please...what is the matter?" Lilli finally asked. Alisz stopped as if surprised by her question.

"It is difficult to centre my thoughts. That is all. So much is about to happen. So many things to remember before you leave," she said, bringing her hands to her temple. "Feverfew! I almost forgot." Pointing toward the bouquet of dried herbs lying on the table, Alisz smiled and motioned for Lilli to start removing the dried leaves.

"Hurry now. I want to give these to your mother to take with her. She will soon be here. We must bag them for your journey. Difficult to say what will be growing in this new land you are off to. You need to prepare for the worst while hoping for the best." Opening several small cloth bags, Alisz filled them with the dried herbs.

"I will miss you terribly once you are gone," she continued. "It has brought me great comfort to have you and, yes, even Friedrich about. Your mother is fortunate to have had children. I regret not having raised a child of my own."

Alisz and her worldly laws, how could she stand back and do nothing? In a flash, the sadness Alisz was fighting hard to disguise crossed her face again. She was trying to be brave, but Lilli knew better. This whole situation was preposterous. Vater was being unreasonable, not even allowing Lilli to express her feelings about the move. If only she could explain to him how she felt...but he cut her off every time she tried to talk about it. And Mutter's attempts to discuss the matter with him had amounted to nothing. Two nights ago, Lilli heard Mutter and Vater talking late at night. Mutter was begging Vater to reconsider.

"It is for the best, Marta," Lilli heard him say. "Once we are settled in the New World, you will see."

The door to the stillroom suddenly opened then, and Mutter and Friedrich stepped in.

"Look what we found," said Mutter, pulling some parsley out of her basket. Friedrich sent Alisz a mischievous smile. Playfully tossing a sprig of the green herb in her direction, he darted across the room, his blond curls bobbing like a duck on a windy pond. Mutter held out her arm, warning him to slow down, but before she could get the words out, he bumped into the table. Several of the jars crashed to the floor. Friedrich hopped out of the way like a startled hare.

"Friedrich! You are like a bull, bumping into everything you see. Oh, look at the mess you have made," Mutter cried. Setting her basket aside, she grabbed the broom and began cleaning up the mess. Friedrich flashed Alisz a frightened look, but the moment he saw the amused look on her face he smiled back.

"It was just an accident," said Alisz, clasping her hands together. "If I had your energy, dear Friedrich, I could surely set the world on fire." He threw his arms around Alisz's waist and held tight. Lilli's heart lurched at the sight of them, and she could not bear to watch.

As the sun lowered itself behind the trees near Alisz's home, Lilli felt a stirring in the pit of her stomach. One more sunset and it would be time for the incantation, to stop this new future that Vater had planned for them all.

"Come now," said Mutter, looking up at the afternoon sky. The sun winked at them from behind the tree branches. "We must go. It is getting late."

Alisz gathered the bags of herbs and put them in Mutter's basket. A torrent of unspoken words passed between them as they looked at one another. Lilli swallowed the lump in her throat. None of this could really be happening. Surely she was caught up in another bad dream. *But where there is life there is hope,* she had heard Alisz say so many times. Once the incantation worked, Vater would wake the next morning and declare that they would be staying.

Lilli was suddenly excited for tomorrow to come, for the moon to rise, and for the incantation to be completed. This was her one last hope, the only chance she had to change the future for all of them.

# CHAPTER TWENTY-ONE

"**Y**OU MUST NOT TELL VATER ABOUT OUR VISIT WITH Alisz. It will only upset him. He would not understand what Alisz does here," Mutter said to Friedrich as they walked home.

"What *does* Alisz do with all those plants?" asked Friedrich with the curiosity of any nine-year-old. Friedrich should not have been allowed into the stillroom. Usually Mutter was careful, but this was to be their last visit with Alisz and they came to say goodbye. Alisz had insisted they be prepared for anything that might arise. The herbs were important. Alisz was adamant that they would need them for the voyage.

"She helps people," said Lilli quickly, hoping her answer would satisfy him. The less he knew about Alisz's practise the better.

"Then why does Vater not like Alisz?" Friedrich asked, kicking at some twigs along the path. Lilli looked at Mutter. It was a question she had often thought of asking herself.

Mutter cleared her throat. "Alisz is different," she said. "That is all you need to know."

Lilli had been uneasy about Friedrich coming to Alisz's with them, but Mutter said it was only fair that Friedrich have the chance to say goodbye as well. As they walked back home, Lilli knew Mutter was right. If something went wrong with the incantation and they indeed had to leave Württemberg, she could not imagine leaving without saying goodbye to Alisz. She expected Friedrich would feel the same.

The day after tomorrow, their journey was set to begin. Alisz had said Lilli should be excited to start a new life in a new land. Lilli wanted to tell her not to worry. With any luck, none of this would be necessary. *Think positive thoughts,* she reminded herself again. Head held high, Lilli imagined Vater telling her that they were staying in Württemberg after all. She could not help but smile.

Walking the beaten path toward home, Lilli was already preparing herself for the incantation, thinking about each step she was about to take. She had never done a spell before, but it did not seem complicated. It was all written down in Alisz's book.

Suddenly, a snake slithered across the path in front of Friedrich, and he raced after it.

"No, Friedrich, leave it be," warned Mutter.

Satisfaction swelled in Lilli's heart as the scaly reptile slipped between the moss-covered rocks. A snake was an omen, a sign of good luck. Smiling, she hurried along. The incantation would work. She was positive.

The following day, Lilli went through her belongings, deciding what to pack in her bag. It felt like a useless gesture. They would not be going anywhere.

"We will not have room for everything. Take only what you absolutely must. Vater will sell the rest before we leave," Mutter said, pausing over her possessions. Lilli felt like an impostor, going though the motions of someone who was planning to depart on a long and arduous journey to the New World. She would share her secret with Mutter only after Vater changed his mind about leaving. And she would tell Alisz, most certainly she would tell Alisz. Alisz was her soul-friend now; she was quick to forgive and understood the failings of the human heart. Alisz would absolve her of any wrongdoing, Lilli was sure of it. If the end result justified the means, all would be forgiven.

That night, as the moon appeared upon the horizon, Lilli slipped out of the house with the items she needed for the incantation hidden in her dress pocket. The full moon would give her plenty of light to work by, but perhaps that was not a good thing. What if someone saw her? Waiting for the Night Goddess to take her chariot across the sky, Lilli made her way toward the shed. She had to work quickly. Crouching in the dirt, she untied the ends of her kerchief. She placed the mugwort in a small cloth bag and took care not to spill any of the contents. Four stands of couch grass and the liquorice root went into the bag. Her trembling hand used a stick to write Vater's name in the dirt—*Karl Eickle*—while she whispered the incantation.

"Let your mind be changed from the path you are taking. As you go toward the future, let your hopes and desires return you to the past. May your heart belong in Württemberg now and forever, so shall it be."

Scooping up the dirt, she placed it all in the bag. As Lilli pulled the string tight, a sigh of relief washed the worry from her. It was done. Crickets chirruped their approval into the warm night air. There was nothing more to do but wait for morning. Her heart was brimming with hope. First the snake crossing her path yesterday and now the crickets chirping—good omens were all about. She stopped to look up at the stars winking down at her. The Night Goddess knew her secret, but she would not tell. Tomorrow everything would be changed; her worries would be behind her.

Rounding the corner of the shed with the charm clutched in her hand, Lilli could already feel the magic working. The house was in darkness. Mutter had not yet returned to light a candle. She had gone to Frau Weber for the evening; a final goodbye before they were to leave. But then, from out of the shadows, a dark figure emerged, startling Lilli to the very core. The hope that had spun within her moments before faded quickly when she saw who it was.

### NEW GERMANY, NOVA SCOTIA, 2019

The website said that the veil between this world and the supernatural was thinnest on Walpurgisnacht. Hopefully, when that night came, Lilly would finally discover why she was having these strange dreams. She'd been trying hard to explain the dreams to Alice, but it was difficult to make her understand.

"The dreams seem like memories, like all this stuff might have really happened. And the woman—it has to be you, Alice. Don't you remember any of the things I told you about?" she said hesitantly. Alice might think she was talking foolishly, yet she needed to know.

"I'm sorry," Alice said, shaking her head. "These are your dreams, Lilly, not mine. There's no way I could remember."

"But you're there. In the dream. We're doing things together. It's like these things really happened a long time ago."

To hide her disappointment, Lilly would turn to her book for comfort. She'd look at the pictures she had drawn when she was small before drifting off to sleep. Again, the dreams would find her. She'd see the cinnamon-haired woman walking deep in the woods. And a young girl, close to her own age, kneeling at the bedside of women writhing in pain. Each time, she'd wake up wondering if the cinnamon-haired woman in her dreams was really Alice, and if it was possible they had known each other in another life.

# CHAPTER TWENTY-TWO

## WÜRTTEMBERG, 1752

"**WHAT WERE YOU DOING OUT THERE, LILLI? WHO WERE** you talking to?" Vater was supposed to be checking the wagon to make sure everything was ready for tomorrow morning. He sounded calm, yet there was anger hidden within his words. Her mind could not think straight, let alone fathom a believable explanation. How long had he been watching her? How long had he been listening?

"Lilli, I asked what you were doing."

"I...I was saying goodbye to our home, to the fields and the trees, that is all."

"Then what is *this*?" he asked, grabbing the cloth bag from her hands.

"No!" she cried, reaching out for it.

Loosening the string, he opened the bag and looked inside.

"Witchcraft!"

"No, Vater! You do not understand."

"I do not understand that my daughter is a *witch*?" This time his voice thundered out across the night. His anger flowed from him like a raging river. Fear stilled Lilli's heart. She could scarcely feel it beating in her chest. Her legs wobbled and the blood rushed from her head. If she tried to run, she would never get away. Vater was too close.

Fear and anger ruptured inside her as she suddenly found her voice. "I am not a witch!" she cried out.

"Then where did you get this? Where?" he said, squeezing the bag in his clenched fist. He emptied its contents, grinding them into the ground with his foot. Throwing the bag down, he grabbed Lilli by both arms. She looked at him, unable to speak. His breath was in her face, his anger so close. Their eyes locked. Then, within the settling darkness, mere inches from her, she saw it in his eyes, heard it in his laboured breathing, between those minute moments of unspoken words. He knew.

"You brought it home from that woman's place, did you not? I knew this would happen. I knew it years ago. When you make a deal with the Devil, you suffer the consequences. I never should have agreed. Never. But Mutter—she thought she knew better."

"Agreed to what?" asked Lilli, between sobs. Vater was not making any sense.

"*That*, you do not need to know."

But she did need to know. It had something to do with Alisz. It had to. All these years Vater had never hid his dislike for her. Each time she went to visit Alisz, she would see the light of disapproval in his eyes. And what had Alisz ever done to him? Nothing, so far as Lilli knew. Fear was his worst enemy. His beliefs, so deeply rooted, would prevent him from ever changing.

Releasing Lilli from his grip, Vater moved with purpose and he started to walk away. His silhouette burned a lasting picture in her mind. Whatever he was planning, she had to stop him.

"Where are you going, Vater?" she cried, running after him. Quickly turning, he grabbed her again, this time leading her toward the shed.

"You need to stay out of this, Lilli. This is not your concern. It is out of your hands now. I am your vater. I will make this better."

"Vater, no!"

Lilli tried to free herself from his grip, but it was no use. Vater was much too strong. She thrust her feet into the earth as he opened the door to the shed. He pushed her inside and she stumbled, falling backwards onto the ground.

"Vater, please…," she begged as he stood braced in the doorway. Tears filled her eyes.

"Believe me—this is for your own good, Lilli. We all make mistakes, but this mistake can be righted."

"What are you going to do? Tell me!"

"What I should have done years ago," he said shutting the door. Jumping to her feet, Lilli pushed against the door to keep it from closing.

"You will thank me later," he said as he fastened the wooden support in place. "Once the witch no longer has a hold on you, you will see that I am right. You will be our Lilli again, not some pawn in this evil witch's plan. 'Thou shall not suffer a witch to live.'"

Complete and utter blackness enveloped her. There was not a fragment of light seeping into the shed. The door rattled as Lilli pounded her fists upon it, crying out to Vater, begging him to free her. She had to get out. Alisz could be in danger. She had to warn her.

*Friedrich!* He had been outside trying to catch a cricket just before dark. Perhaps he was nearby. She called out to him, beating upon the door, hoping he would hear and set her free. But there came no answer. A deluge of tears flowed from her. She had to get out if she wanted to save Alisz from Vater's wrath. Desperation lowered her to her knees. Just when she thought she would never be free, the door swung open.

"Vater?" she cried out. Perhaps he had come back to let her out.

"Lilli, what are you doing in here?" Mutter reached down and helped her to her feet.

"Hurry, we have to warn Alisz!" Lilli cried, grabbing Mutter's hand.

"Warn Alisz about what? You are not making sense."

"Vater. He said he never should have agreed."

"What are you talking about, Lilli?"

The cool night air waited for her answer. The leaves on the rowan tree whispered for her to tell. A sliver of moonlight looked out from behind a thin veil of wispy clouds. There was no point in pretending otherwise. The truth was there for the world to see. Lilli could not deny it. She saw a trace of bewilderment spread across Mutter's face as the truth found a place on her lips.

"I am the fox, Mutter—the fox in Alisz's dream."

# CHAPTER
# TWENTY-THREE

"**F**RIEDRICH!" CALLED MUTTER, HURRYING TOWARD THE house as twilight continued to lower her curtain earthward. "Friedrich, come quick!"

"Vater would not have left Friedrich alone. He must have taken him," said Lilli. "I'm certain of it. I called and called for him, but he did not answer."

"Come then, we must hurry," said Mutter, taking Lilli by the hand. The wind whipped the words from her, leaving them scattered into the dark like fireflies. Fear hung in the air, flitting back and forth like an injured bird. The western sky appeared bruised and battered. Crimson hues lay across the horizon, torn and stretched. Trees in the distance opened their shadowy branches, inviting danger into their waiting arms. Lilli wanted to forget this night ever happened. But there was no hiding from this. Alisz was in danger. Lilli was the one who had put her in danger, and she had to help.

As they hurried toward Alisz's home, Lilli looked up at the moon rising high in the sky. A silvery halo bulged from its circular face. She tried to remember all the things Alisz had told her over the years about the moon's special powers, but she could not think of a single thing. Just like the bulging moon, her mind also swelled with thoughts of what Vater would do if they did not get to Alisz in time. She could not concentrate at all.

The moon lit their way in the dark until they came to the shadowy footpath that would lead them directly to the stillroom door. Lilli had used the path at night many times, knew every hole and rock and twig along the way. As they turned off the road, Mutter hesitated.

"It will be all right," said Lilli. She would not let herself think about stumbling in the dark. Her feet knew the way, they always had. She would allow them to take the lead. But as they neared Alisz's home, Lilli realized they were too late. A large bonfire was burning not far from Alisz's house. Flames skipped in the breeze, lighting the darkness. An angry mob had surrounded the fire, shouting and banging sticks on the ground. Some were ringing ox bells as if it were Walpurgisnacht. Lilli brought her hands to her ears. The noise rose up in great bursts, so loud that she could scarcely hear herself think.

"Will they hurt her?" she asked, desperately needing some reassurance from Mutter.

"I pray not. But when fearful people come together, there is no telling what they will do."

They remained at a safe distance, removed from the crowd. Lilli looked about but could not find anyone in the dark resembling Vater. He had to be here somewhere. He was the one responsible for this, she was sure of it. There was no other explanation. When a boy darted out from the shadows raising a stick in the air, Lilli turned toward Mutter, confused.

"That is Friedrich," she whispered. "But why?" Alisz was his friend. They laughed together about silly things. How could Friedrich be a part of this?

"It is the crowd. It feeds off fear. Friedrich is too young to know," said Mutter, shaking her head.

Flames licked the night—yellow, red, orange—flickering and spitting into the dark. Men began to throw sticks into the flames, feeding the fire as it begged, more, more! Heat touched Lilli's face as the chants from the crowd grew stronger, louder. A great force surrounded them, a powerful energy that beat with a pulse of its own. It hovered in the air above them. It poked and prodded its gnarly fingers. The mob continued their cruelty, throwing stones at Alisz's home, crying for her to come out. Lilli and Mutter remained in the shadows, hiding among the trees.

"Come out, witch!" It was Vater's voice. Lilli looked quickly at Mutter. Before this night, Lilli would never have thought Vater capable of such cruel acts. But there he was, raising his fist and leading the chants. What had come over him? Terror squeezed her heart as she forced air into her lungs. It was almost unbearable. Tears streamed down her face. Flames danced, taunting the angry mob, daring them to take more drastic action. It was Lilli's fault. How simple she thought it would be to change Vater's mind with an incantation. She should have listened to Alisz. How foolish she had been.

"Burn her!" someone else cried, and the crowd picked up the call.

*"Burn the witch...burn the witch...burn the witch,"* came the chant. Someone tall and broad stepped forward and reached into the fire with a stick. Pulling it back out, it was a glowing blaze, matted and twisted in flames.

*"Burn the witch...burn the witch..."*

The chanting grew louder as the fire-bearer walked toward Alisz's house with the torch raised high. Vater was in the crowd. Why did he not put a stop to this? The thatch roof on Alisz's cottage would ignite immediately. If Alisz was inside she would be trapped. Lilli had to do something. She had to make them stop.

"No...leave her be. She has done nothing wrong!" cried Lilli in earnest, moving out from the safety of the trees. Her words were sent hurling into the crowd.

"Lilli, no," whispered Mutter, grabbing her by the arm. But it was too late. Heads turned and people stopped moving. For a few moments, the crowd fell to near silence. There was only the soft murmuring of a few voices that slowly waned away to nothing. The breeze hesitated. The leaves on the trees ceased their rustling. Time paused, as the forced stillness became woven into the fabric of the night sky.

"Who spoke in the witch's defence?" someone shouted. Lilli was certain it was Vater.

"Who was that?"

"Who wants to save the witch?"

"We must go, Lilli. We must go before they find us out," said Mutter in desperation.

"But we have to stay and help!"

"There *is* no help here, Lilli. There is nothing we can do. It is too late. We can only hope that Alisz is someplace safe."

"But we leave tomorrow. We will never know."

"Faith, Lilli. You need to have faith," said Mutter, taking her hand.

They made their escape down the same narrow path that had lead them there. Behind them, the crowd began to prattle until they were shouting and jeering once again.

*"Burn the witch! Burn the witch!"*

Lilli had no choice but to consider the truth in Mutter's words; faith was the only way she could endure not knowing the truth. She reached for the pendant around her neck. Alisz had said the rainbow moonstone had special powers that would join them together. Surely, Lilli would feel if Alisz were in danger. Alisz was wise, a master of understanding the signs that came her way. Alisz would look to the sky, to the plants, to the earth, to keep herself safe from harm—or would she?

"Keep moving and do not look back," said Mutter. When they were far enough away that they could no longer make out what the crowd was shouting, they stopped to rest.

"Vater said he had made a deal with the Devil," said Lilli, breathlessly turning toward Mutter. "I must know what he meant."

"It is a complicated story, Lilli. One that would be difficult for you to understand."

"But I want to know," whispered Lilli.

"I have made a vow not to speak of certain things," said Mutter softly.

"Please," Lilli implored. "Please tell me. Is it my story? Can you at least tell me that?"

Mother closed her eyes and nodded. Moonlight flickered through the treetops as she released a heavy sigh.

"We have no time for this, Lilli. We must go home before Vater returns. Now come."

# CHAPTER
# TWENTY-FOUR

A S SOON AS THEY ARRIVED BACK HOME, LILLI REMOVED her wrap and hurried to light a candle. Her heart ached in her chest. She could not stop wondering if Alisz was safe or whether she had been trapped inside the flames of her burning house. How would she leave tomorrow without knowing the truth? Mutter told her she needed to have faith, but faith was more than a spoken word. It was a belief. A belief so strong it fills you with a knowing that all is well and offers you peace at the same time. Most times, belief in what seems like the impossible does not come about easily, as Mutter often told her. But how would this faith Mutter spoke of sustain her over the months and years ahead? And yet, at the moment, it was all Lilli had left to cling to. No one she knew was as wise and resourceful as Alisz. The Goddess *would* protect her—she had to have faith.

One thing Lilli was certain about: she would never forgive Vater for his part in all of it. He was the one responsible for setting it all in motion, she was sure of it. He'd allowed his fears to rule his heart. How could he be so cruel to Alisz? She thought of the first time she'd returned from assisting Alisz at a birth, how proud he had seemed.

But now, through her own actions, she had put Alisz's life in jeopardy. If only Lilli had listened to Alisz and had not tried to interfere with the path fate had set out for her. Who was she to question the natural order of things? Alisz had told her many times that life unfolds as it is meant to and that there is no point in fighting against the things that are meant to be.

Lilli and Mutter were barely settled in when a gentle knock came at the back door.

"Who could it be?" Lilli asked. It was too late in the evening for company. Mutter looked at Lilli and held her finger to her lips. She took up the candle and went to the door. Lilli followed, her heart beating wildly in her chest. She held her breath. If someone had followed them from Alisz's, they could be in grave trouble. They might be accused of defending a witch or even accused of being witches themselves. There was little difference between the two, to those who believed.

"Who is it?" Mutter whispered mere inches from the door.

"Please, open the door. It is I, Alisz."

*Alisz!* Glee leaped inside Lilli's chest as she and Mutter shared a look of relief. Mutter reached for the latch and the door flung open in the wind. The night breeze accompanied Alisz though the doorway. Her hair hung down in ribbons, matted and windblown. Behind the flaming candle in Mutter's hand, Alisz's eyes glowed the colour of the sea. Throwing her arms around Alisz, Lilli held tight.

"We were so worried," said Lilli. "We saw the flames. We—" But she stopped, suddenly ashamed that she was the one responsible for setting it all in motion. Alisz's chest was rising and falling as she gasped for air. Opening her wrap, she pulled her herb book out from between the folds of material.

"I want you to have this, Lilli," she said, holding the book out for Lilli to take.

She could not possibly accept such a gift. It should be passed down to a family member. What if Alisz were to one day have a child?

"No, Alisz, I cannot. It is yours. Surely there is someone else more worthy."

"Please, Lilli. You are the only one. I am entrusting it to you. Take it with you to your new home. Continue the work you started here. It is the only way I know it will be safe."

A sob filled with both yearning and regret passed Lilli's lips as Alisz pressed the book in her hands. She had longed to possess such a book since she first laid eyes on it and even dreamed one day of starting her own. Never once had she imagined Alisz would give her this one, and certainly never under these circumstances.

"The drawings," she managed to squeeze out between her trembling lips. "All the lovely drawings. And the recipes. How will you remember?"

"I can always make another book. As for the cures, many of them are imprinted in my memory. This book is meant for you. You must not give in to worry. Worry does not solve a thing. Trust that I will be fine."

The stillroom book was Alisz's most prized position, passed down by the women in her family, their wisdom, their history, the very soul of who they were and their practise of medicine. It would not be right for her to give it away.

"I am not family," Lilli argued.

Alisz laid her hand on Lilli's. "You have been my family these past eight years. Together we have laughed and shared many things. That is the true meaning of family."

"But it is my fault. I tried to change Vater's mind about leaving. None of this would have happened otherwise." It was impossible to look Alisz in the eyes. Yet she had to own the role she had played in all of this, even if it meant Alisz would be unable to forgive her.

Alisz stopped a tear from trickling down Lilli's face. "We are not responsible for the actions of another," she said. "Remember St. Hildegard's words, Lilli: 'Even in a world that is being shipwrecked, remain brave and strong.'" Lilli looked up at Alisz and saw only forgiveness.

Holding Alisz's book in her grip, Lilli wished that between the oily covers there was a cure for all the fear and ignorance in the world, something that would stop people from accusing one another of witchcraft.

A tight smile stretched across Alisz's lips. "There is no reason to cry, dear Lilli. Life unfolds as it is meant to. You will see this one day. You are a strong girl. All will be fine...you will be fine. I am sure of it."

"Where will you go?" asked Mutter, concern dampening her words.

"I have a safe place," said Alisz. "You must not worry. In time, people will forget their fear. Life in Württemberg will become safe again. Now, you must be brave—both of you."

"You should go now, before you are discovered," said Mutter, moving toward the door. As much as she longed to have Alisz stay, Lilli knew Mutter was right. Vater could be home at any time.

"Wait!" cried Lilli, removing the pendant from around her neck. "Take this, my soul-friend. I will never forget you." Lilli sobbed as Alisz slipped the pendant over her head. "No matter what, I will never forget."

"Of course not, my dear sweet lily-of-the-valley, and neither will I. This is not the last time we will be together. We will find each other in another life—in another place and another time. The rainbow moonstone will connect us when the time is right," she said. "It is not for us to know when, for that part we have no control over."

Hugging both Mutter and Lilli one last time, Alisz turned toward the door. As she disappeared into the dark veil of night, Lilli made a silent vow to guard Alisz's precious book with her life.

⌒

### NEW GERMANY, 2019

"My time here is short, dear sweet lily-of-the valley. I have said we would meet again in another place and another time. That time is coming. It will be up to you to awaken our past memories, or they will be lost."

"Up to me?" Lilly didn't want anything to be up to her, especially something as important as this sounded.

"There is a small window of opportunity and then it will be gone," continued the cinnamon-haired woman.

"But what? When?"

"Walpurgisnacht. It is when the veil is thinnest. We are soul-friends, and when the time is right, you must act if you want to awaken our memories in this present time."

"What do I do?" Lilly begged, desperate to know more.

"When the time is right, you will know what to do," said the cinnamon-haired woman before she faded away.

"But wait! What's a soul-friend?" Lilly cried out in her dream, but it was no use. The cinnamon-haired woman was gone.

Lilly sat up in bed. She hurried to the computer and typed in *soul-friend*.

"A soul friend is someone you feel you have known in a past life and that you agreed to meet up with again in another lifetime."

Lilly's heart beat fast. That was it! That was exactly how she felt about the cinnamon-haired woman. In her dream, she said Lilly would know what to do. But what did that mean? There were instructions on the site for performing a soul-friend ceremony.

Maybe that would awaken their memories. But to do that, Lilly would have to convince Alice that she really was the cinnamon-haired woman from her dreams, that they had been soul-friends a long time ago.

# CHAPTER
# TWENTY-FIVE

## SAILING TOWARD ROTTERDAM ON THE RHINE, 1752

**T**INY JEWELS OF SUNLIGHT DANCED ON THE WATER IN THE early morning. Lilli watched the waves moving merrily up and down but refused to feel any gaiety inside. Vater had paid for their passage and they were waiting their turn to board the raft that would take them down the Rhine to the city of Rotterdam. Standing as still as a statue, she watched the raft filling with people. Some of the faces she recognized from the market she and Mutter sometimes walked to, others were completely unknown to her. The one thing they all had in common was their desire to start a new life on the other side of the world. But what did the future actually hold for any of them? Lilli's eyes filled with tears and she quickly brushed them away. Tears would change nothing.

"Hurry along," said one of the raftsmen as he motioned for people to speed up. Friedrich was the first to step aboard the log raft while Vater struggled to bring the large trunk that held their possessions. *What a paltry amount*, thought Lilli as she watched him dragging the trunk behind him. To think that their lives had been reduced to such meagreness only deepened her sadness. So many of the things she loved had been sold off before they left. What personal belongings she held close to her heart were in the bag she now carried with her. She had packed Alisz's book last so that it would be close by. Reaching down, she could feel the outline of the covers beneath her fingertips.

As Mutter paused and set her bag down on the riverbank, Lilli held her breath. It was not too late for her to speak up and tell Vater she would not go. She looked back over her shoulder as if trying to decide what to do. Lilli studied the lines on Mutter's face, realizing that she had not seen her smile in many weeks. Would she refuse to board the raft? When Mutter reached for her bag, Lilli's heart sank.

Vater insisted they sit on the trunk together, even though there was not much room. He was afraid of becoming separated from it and losing what little they had. Mutter settled down beside him, clutching her bag close. From the riverbank, the breeze challenged Lilli to step aboard. For a split second she considered running off, letting her family go down the Rhine without her. But where would she go? She would be all alone with no idea how to get home. Besides, there was nothing left at home for her. Everything had been sold. She could not even seek out asylum with Alisz.

"Quickly, Lilli. Sit down beside Mutter," said Vater sternly. Lilli gave him a vile look. After what he'd done to Alisz, she would never speak to him again. She quickly glanced at Mutter. The look she sent Lilli begged her to comply with Vater's wishes. She squeezed over to allow Lilli a small place while Friedrich climbed onto Vater's lap. Alisz would tell her she must learn to embrace the changes that have come her way, but Lilli was not sure that was possible.

She continued to cling to a small thread of hope that their voyage would come to an end before they boarded the ship. Stepping reluctantly onto the raft, Lilli silently prayed for the Goddess to bring this voyage to an end.

$\infty$

"The river is so long. When will we reach the sea?" asked Friedrich when they stopped at the first way station. It was as if he expected that Holland was no farther away than a trip to the market.

"Patience," said Vater. "You must be patient. We have weeks to go before we even reach Rotterdam."

"Is that where the big ship is?"

Vater nodded. "Yes, that is where the big ship is waiting." When Friedrich frowned, Vater added, "I did not promise that this would be a short journey." As Vater stared off into space, Lilli could see the excitement gleaming in his eyes. He was as anxious as Friedrich to start this new life with no care at all what she and Mutter were feeling.

The trip down the Rhine was long and cramped with so many people crowded onto the raft together. Mutter spent many hours with her head bowed in silent prayer, urging Lilli to do the same.

Lilli clutched fast to her bag as they drifted downriver. Seeking some comfort from home, she would trace the outline of Alisz's book with her fingers. She knew that Alisz would tell her to enjoy the journey, for there were many new sights. But as they went past castles and tall church steeples on their way to Rotterdam, Lilli stubbornly refused to acknowledge the beauty before her. Looking at the faces around her, she wondered how many of the other travellers were as unhappy as she.

Vater complained about the high prices for the supplies he picked up at some of the many stops along the way. Whenever they stopped, a toll had to be paid in order for them to continue down the river. Each time Vater had to put out more money, Mutter looked on with gravity. They had not even made it down the Rhine and their money was quickly disappearing. If this kept up, how would they possibly pay for their passage across the ocean? Mutter whispered to Vater. Lilli prayed they would be turned away before they made it out to sea. But as the days brought them closer to Rotterdam, the hope Lilli was clinging to slipped slowly away. It did not look as though her prayers were about to be answered.

Rotterdam was busy and noisy. Lilli had never seen so many people in one place. They were ushered into a small shed. Vater sat at a table and signed papers for their passage to the New World. And then the day came when they were to board the ship that would take them across the ocean to Nova Scotia. It was then Lilli finally accepted that there was no turning back.

# CHAPTER TWENTY-SIX

"**M**OVE ALONG, MOVE ALONG," VATER URGED AS HE pushed Friedrich through the crowd of passengers. The ship was not about to sail without them. Lilli wished Vater was not so eager to be leaving. She gasped when she saw the vessel that was to take them to the next leg of their journey. The ship's gigantic mast reached out to the dark grey clouds hanging overhead. It was a dreary sight that mimicked the feelings inside her.

A flurry of feet vibrated against the wharf as people rushed toward the gangplank the moment it was lowered. People were shouting and laughing, excited to be heading into a brand new life. Friedrich let out a squeal, clapping his hands as he jumped up and down. He suddenly bolted past Mutter and she reached out to stop him, barely skimming the top of his head as he raced by. She called out for him to slow down, but he did not heed her words.

"Go after your bruder, Lilli," ordered Vater as Friedrich's blond curls disappeared into the sea of strangers. Clutching fast to her belongings, Lilli weaved her way among the passengers, calling out for Friedrich to stop, but her bag was burdensome and it was difficult to hurry. Friedrich slipped through the crowd like a hungry weasel. If he heard Lilli cry out to him, he did not let on. Just as she caught sight of him again, she stumbled, and her bag flew from her hands, nearly striking a woman in front of her. "Forgive me," gasped Lilli, catching herself moments before falling flat on her face. "My bruder, he has run off. I am trying to catch him."

In the woman's arms was a young child. Two older children were hanging fast to her skirt, eyes wide with wonder. One had a thumb stuck in her mouth, the other was softly whining. Lilli could only imagine they were as frightened by the unknown as she was.

"It is a good day to be chasing after an adventure," said the woman with a gleam in her eyes. "If only we all had his liveliness." *If only indeed*, thought Lilli, annoyed that Friedrich had run off the way he did. The woman seemed happy and appeared nearly as excited as Friedrich, even with a passel of young children holding fast to her. And what of the child she was carrying, Lilli wondered, taking notice of her large, round midsection. Was she not at all concerned?

"Come along, Minna," said a man, turning toward them. The children ran quickly toward him. "I am sure we will see each other later," said Minna, smiling at Lilli. Lilli picked up her bag and hurried off to find Friedrich again. When she finally closed in on him, she made a mad leap and caught him by the arm.

"You are hurting me!" he said, swatting at his sister, but she was not about to release him from her grasp.

"Vater sent me to get you," hissed Lilli, pulling him back through the crowd.

"We must not become separated," whispered Mutter, twisting Friedrich's ear as she led him along. "If you get lost in the crowd it could take hours to find you. We will need to show proof of our passage."

As she boarded the ship, Lilli refused to look back over her shoulder, even though she longed to with all her heart. As strongly as she felt about leaving, her future was no longer back there. She had to focus, with every ounce of willpower she had, on the voyage ahead. *We all do things we do not want to.* Alisz's words followed her like a haunting melody.

## NEW GERMANY, NOVA SCOTIA, 2019

"Please be home," whispered Lilly as she stood outside Alice's house. She knocked again. There was a small light deep inside. She couldn't tell if Alice was home or not. Why hadn't she called ahead of time? Alice could be anywhere. It was Saturday night. Walpurgisnacht. When the veil between the worlds was thinnest. She wouldn't get another chance. The cinnamon-haired woman had said it was up to her to awaken their memories. Desperation threatened to overtake Lilly as she stood outside Alice's door. What would she do if Alice wasn't home? She knocked once again, harder this time. Seconds later, she heard footsteps heading her way. She sighed with relief. It wasn't too late.

Alice's voice rang out musically when the door opened. "What a wonderful surprise, Lilly. Did you want to come in?" Lilly nodded. "It is late for a visit. Does your mother know you're here?"

"Yes," lied Lilly. "She said it was okay. It's important." Her parents had been watching a movie when she'd slipped out of the house. They thought she was in her room.

"What do you have there?" Alice asked as Lilly stepped inside and slipped off her backpack.

"Promise you won't laugh?" said Lilly as she followed Alice into her small living room.

"When have I ever laughed at you?"

"All the time. That's what you do, you laugh a lot." Lilly kneeled beside the coffee table and beckoned for Alice to do the same.

"I suppose you're right," she said, following Lilly's directions. "Okay. I promise not to laugh this time. If you show me what you have."

"Patience," said Lilly smiling, something Alice often said to her. "I had another dream."

"Oh, Lilly, not another one. I hope it wasn't upsetting. You look upset."

Lilly swallowed. "You remember the woman I've been dreaming about, the one who looks like you? She told me something last night."

"You said you couldn't communicate with her, that she speaks a different language."

"I know that's what I said, but last night I could. I could understand everything she said." Lilly stopped when she saw the doubt on Alice's face. It was useless. There was no way she could make Alice understand what she didn't fully understand herself.

She moved in close to Alice. She'd have to try a different approach. "Do you trust me?" she said.

Alice patted Lilly's hand. "Of course I trust you. I've known you a long time. You are not one to make up extravagant stories."

"Then there is something I need you to do, no questions, no words."

"No questions or words? None? You are being mysterious." Alice pulled her shoulders back and folded her hands in her lap. "Okay. Whatever you say. Now, show me what you have."

Lilly removed the items from her backpack and placed them on the coffee table. First, she laid out a cloth runner. She put the candles in the holders and asked Alice to light them. The site had said to use three goblets, but since her mother didn't have any, wine glasses would have to do. There were two small glasses and a larger one, and Lilly placed them on the runner between the two candles. Alice raised an eyebrow.

"No questions, remember?" said Lilly. Removing the Thermos of herbal tea, she poured some into the two smaller glasses. The last item she took from her backpack was the book with the blank pages Alice had given her when she was five. She had wrapped it in bright red paper and fastened a pretty white and red polka dot ribbon on it. Her gift to Alice. The website said that gifts could be exchanged.

Once the candles were lit, Lilly began.

"As I was saying, last night the woman who looks just like you came to me in a dream. She said that we are soul-friends. I looked that up and it's someone you knew from a past life and that you've agreed to meet again."

"Who do you think this woman in your dream is, Lilly? And what does that have to do with all this?" said Alice, indicating the items spread before them.

"Don't you see? The dreams I've been having, they're things that really and truly happened in a past life. We knew each other before. Right now they're just dreams, but I think I've found a way for us to remember. Alice, you're the cinnamon-haired woman—or at least you were."

Alice started to speak.

"Please don't say anything," said Lilly. "No questions, remember? I know this all sounds crazy, but all those dreams have to mean something. How could I dream about Walpurgisnacht when I've never heard of it before?" Lilly paused, searching for the right words. "Please trust me," she said. "Tonight is April thirtieth—Walpurgisnacht. The veil between the worlds is supposed to be the thinnest. You said," Lilly paused, "I mean, the cinnamon-haired woman said she'd promised we'd meet again in another lifetime. This is that other lifetime."

"Lilly..." Alice was shaking her head. There was a sad look on her face. How would Lilly ever get through to her? This was their only chance to discover who they were in another lifetime, and for Lilly to find meaning in the dreams. What if, after tonight, all the things she'd been dreaming about were forgotten, the same way the memories she'd had when she was small had been lost? They would never reunite their bond of friendship, and would never recognize each other from this other lifetime. When Walpurgisnacht was over, it would all be too late. There had to be some way to make Alice understand.

# CHAPTER
# TWENTY-SEVEN

ATLANTIC OCEAN, 1752

ONCE THEY WERE OUT ON THE OCEAN, LILLI OVERHEARD Vater tell Mutter that he did not have the money for their passage.

"The papers I signed in Rotterdam, it was an agreement with the British. We will work for them until the entire debt is paid. There was no other way. But it will be fine, you will see. There are many others in this same situation."

"Karl, you have sold your family, and for what?" Mutter whispered. "Who knows what will await us in this new land—if we even make it there?"

"You are worried for nothing," said Vater. "We will make it to our destination. Many already have." Vater's words were filled with confidence, yet the doubt in Mutter's voice struck a chord in Lilli. What *would* be waiting for them in Nova Scotia? She cursed the British and their offer of help. Why could they not leave well enough alone? Why were they so anxious to uproot families, to send people off to this unsettled land? Who was to say they could be trusted?

"We owned nothing in Württemberg, Marta, not a single plot of land, and you know very well the other reason we could not stay. Lilli was being influenced. Trouble was on the way. I warned you. I warned you in the beginning not to let that woman near our Lilli," said Vater, his voice rising in anger. Lilli could not believe Vater was using Alisz as an excuse for their leaving home when it was clear that he had been lured by the promise of owning land.

Vater grunted when Mutter whispered for him to keep his voice down.

"We had an agreement with Alisz," said Mutter, speaking quietly.

"*We* also had an agreement—you and I. *We* agreed that Lilli would never know, that it was in her best interest. I do not care about some agreement *you* made with that woman." Vater spoke with passion, his voice climbing.

"And I did not break my word to you, Karl. It is as we agreed."

"And what about *her*? What might *she* have told Lilli?"

"Alisz would never."

Lilli could stand it no longer. She stepped out from the shadows. She had to know what they were talking about. "What was I never to know?" she asked, breaking her silence with Vater. She had not spoken to him since the night he had led the angry mob to Alisz's cottage.

"Lilli!" Mutter gasped spinning around to face her. "How long have you been listening?"

"This is your fault, Marta," said Vater, his face pulled tight in anger.

"Vater, please...please tell me," implored Lilli as he stormed across the deck and away from her. She looked toward Mutter. "What was I never to know?" she demanded again, this time staring directly into Mutter's eyes.

"It is a story that changes nothing about the outcome," said Mutter. "Just know that some things are best kept private. This is one of those things."

Day and night the ship creaked and groaned. Sleep did not come easily for Lilli, for it was constantly interrupted by the rocking back and forth and the mournful sounds that squeaked out from between the weathered timbers. As she lay awake in the dark, she could hear mumbled voices long into the night. Although she could not often make out what was being said, the sounds prevented her from settling into a deep slumber. From somewhere inside the crowded hull came the sobs of a woman, low and strained, throughout most of the night, but after the first week she stopped.

Each morning, Lilli placed a mark inside Alisz's book to keep track of the passing days. *How long will it take for us to reach land?* she wondered, as seven days slowly turned into fourteen, then twenty-one, with still no end in sight. Every day Lilli counted the marks, hoping she would discover that the number had miraculously doubled or tripled over night and they were closer to their destination. She knew the length of the voyage would depend greatly upon the weather. If the winds did not fill their sails as it should, they could very well drift about aimlessly, while a fierce storm might send them far off course. Both could add days or weeks to their voyage.

When the other children went off to explore the vessel, Lilli kept to herself. She would sometimes open the stillroom book and try to distinguish the images in the dim light inside the ship.

She would then test her knowledge of herbs by going over some of the cures in her mind—willow bark for fever; chamomile for digestion and sleep, feverfew for relieving headache, stress, and inflammation; raspberry leaf for easing the pain of childbirth. It would be important to know these things once she arrived in the New World. She would not have Alisz there to ask questions.

"Come up on deck," Mutter coaxed one day. "We are having another prayer meeting." Lilli sometimes heard Mutter praying during the night even when it was not stormy, and most days she went up to the deck with some of the other women to pray for their safe arrival in the New World.

"Do you think God approves of our leaving Württemberg?" Lilli asked, but Mutter did not answer.

"Can you not find yourself a friend on board this big ship?" Mutter asked Lilli one day. "It will make the time go faster. You need to let go of your misery."

"Why would I want to make a friend?" said Lilli fervently. "So that we can say goodbye once we reach land?" Lilli had no need for ordinary friends. She had a soul-friend, and that friendship would last for this lifetime and beyond.

One day, when she could no longer stand to be confined to the darkness, Lilli wandered up on the deck for some fresh air. There were many people standing about, taking in the air and sunshine. A sudden burst of laughter reached her ears and she looked toward the sound. A number of children were racing around the deck playing tag, Friedrich among them. On the far side of the deck, Mutter and Vater were in deep conversation with a couple who had travelled down the Rhine with them, and they did not see her when she crawled up from down below. For that Lilli was glad. She did not know what she would say to Vater anyway. Knowing that he insisted that Mutter keep secrets from her only deepened her anger.

The breeze tugged and pulled at her as she stood looking out across the endless horizon. There was not a tree, much less a leaf, in sight. Sunlight sparkled on the crest of the waves and for a brief moment her spirits lifted. She even dared wonder if this new world they were sailing off to would have some of the same healing plants that grew back home in Württemberg. But just as that small spark of hope began to pulse brighter, Lilli pulled back, reminding herself that this new land was not Württemberg and never would be.

"Life can send us in many different directions in the course of just one lifetime," Alisz had told her before she left. "Remember to keep an open mind. Do not compare the things you had with the things you *will* have. They are not the same, but both can be equally good. Always look ahead, Lilli, and do not long for what has been left behind." Not looking back was more difficult than it sounded. There were sure to be many differences in this new land, and it might not resemble Württemberg in any way. But what if Alisz was mistaken? What if she did not find any good in the New World? It was something she needed to prepare for.

A brisk wind whipped around the bow of the ship. Lilli pulled her arms across her body for warmth. She looked around at the passengers out on the deck, old people, young people, men, women, and children, and she felt suddenly alone. Again her thoughts turned toward Alisz. She found herself wondering about this safe place Alisz had gone to.

"I am glad to see that you finally found your way up to the deck." Minna's sudden appearance startled Lilli. The young children were still clinging to her, eyes now dark and hollow, and the child in her arms was whining.

Lilli looked at Minna and forced a smile. "It is so dark down there," she said. "I missed the sunshine."

"I have been looking for you every day," said Minna. She hooked a stray lock of hair behind Lilli's ear. The young child in her arms squirmed to be released and she let him down onto the deck to run around.

"Keep watch over Stefan, and do not get too close to the railing or you will fall overboard," she told the oldest girl, who did not seem old enough to look out for herself, let alone a child barely able to walk.

"When will your child be born?" Lilli asked.

"I am hoping it will wait until we reach land, but I overheard someone say that a storm could take us off course and our trip could take much longer." Lilli silently prayed that would not be the case. Minna paused and looked out across the endless waves. Concern stretched across her face. As she turned toward Lilli, tears formed in her eyes.

"For now, I am trying not to think of all the things that could go wrong." Minna smiled, but Lilli was not fooled. Behind the pleasant exterior she was showing others, fear and sadness were hiding. "I have heard there is no surgeon onboard," Minna added.

"Do not worry," said Lilli touching the girl's hand. "If your time comes while you are on the ship, I can help."

Minna looked at her doubtfully. "You are not very old," she said. "What could you possibly do?"

"In Württemberg I worked with a midwife. There are things I know. I could help...that is, if you should need me," she added.

"That is very kind of you," said Minna. She sighed. "I wanted to wait until the child was born, but Hans was afraid the boats might stop sailing and the land grants would be gone."

"We do not always get the thing we want," said Lilli, looking out across the wide expanse.

༄

In the quiet of the evening, Lilli overheard Vater making plans with some of the other men. They spoke about owning their own plot of land, raising crops and animals, and building homes from nothing.

On clear, warm nights, Vater and Friedrich slept out on the deck beneath the night sky with many of the other passengers. Lilli and Mutter remained cramped in the dark in a space scarcely large enough for the two of them, let alone Vater and Friedrich. Although the air inside the berth was suffocating, Lilli knew she could not bear to look up at the same moon that was shining down on Württemberg. At night, she rested her head on Alisz's book with thoughts of home pressed deeply in her mind.

### NEW GERMANY, NOVA SCOTIA, 2019

Lilly reached for her backpack and unzipped the small pocket in front. She took out a folded piece of paper with instructions for the soul-friend ceremony. She and Alice each took a sip of herbal tea and, exchanging glasses, drank once again.

"This bigger glass represents a unity chalice." Lilly poured her remaining tea into it, telling Alice to do the same. The flickering candles cast small shadows on the wall behind Alice. Lilly handed her the paper with the words she had found on the internet.

"I will go first," she said. "Just read what is on your paper. When we are done, we'll take turns drinking from the unity glass." She took a deep breath and began.

"I am your friend," said Lilly.

Alice hesitated, but eventually replied, "I am also your friend." Slowly, they went through the steps of the soul-friend ceremony. Next, they poured their tea into the unity goblet and each took a drink. What would it feel like to suddenly remember a past life? In the moments that followed, Lilly waited anxiously for a transformation, but nothing came.

"Do you feel any different?" she asked. Alice shook her head. "Me neither." Suddenly she remembered the gift she'd brought and handed it to Alice. Perhaps the book would jar something loose. That had to be it!

"It's the book I gave you when you were small!" Alice sounded delighted. Slowly opening the cover, she looked at Lilly's drawings from years ago. Lilly eagerly waited for something unusual to happen—exactly what, she wasn't sure. The cinnamon-haired woman had said that when the time was right, she'd know what to do. But nothing she'd done so far had unlocked any memories.

Maybe Alice was right. What she'd been experiencing were just dreams. There really were no memories. Maybe the dreams meant nothing at all, except that she had a very active imagination. She'd done everything the site said to do, but she didn't feel any different.

Lilly bit back her disappointment. She'd been wrong; the soulfriend ceremony had failed. She hadn't known Alice in another lifetime. She'd been foolish to think she had. It was the false memories Alice had spoken of, and Lilly had convinced herself they were true.

# CHAPTER
# TWENTY-EIGHT

"**W**HEN WILL WE REACH THE NEW WORLD? I AM TIRED of the dark, smelly ship."

Lilli did not want to hear any more of Friedrich's endless laments. All along he was the one who had been so excited to set sail across the sea. But now that the adventure had grown old, he no longer wanted a part in it.

"Go off and play," Vater ordered when he could no longer stand the sound of Friedrich's whining. Friedrich disappeared with some of the others boys his age, returning many hours later, tired and hungry yet scarcely picking at the barley and rice Mutter gave him to eat. Lilli couldn't blame him. What she wouldn't give for a fresh loaf of bread. The food on the ship was ghastly. Even with the hunger she felt, she dreaded the thought of mealtime. Not once since boarding had they eaten a palatable meal. Even the sweet, sticky treacle Mutter added did not make the food appetizing. Lilli looked down at the rice and barley with small bits of salt meat. In time her stomach would stop feeling empty. If only Mutter did not insist she eat at least a few mouthfuls for each meal.

"I know it is bad, Lilli, but it is all we have," Mutter would say, picking gingerly at the food.

"I would rather eat a dead rat."

"Do not say such things," scolded Mutter. "We need to be thankful for what we *do* have regardless of what that is. The Lord will provide for us, but we have to meet Him halfway."

The water that had been brought onboard for the journey was stale and murky. Vinegar was added to it, but still it did not make it palatable. Lilli forced herself to drink small sips only when her thirst became too much to bear. When the rain came, Mutter set a pot on deck to collect fresh rainwater. Far worse than the meals and the water were the buckets with human waste they were forced to use, with little privacy. People were constantly seasick, retching the contents of their stomach into the same buckets. The smell that filled the ship's hold was overpowering. Each day, Vater would climb through the hatch with their bucket and dump it over the side of the ship.

Lilli was still angry with Vater and refused to speak to him. If he noticed her anger, he did not let on. She could not stop thinking about the horrible atrocities he'd shouted outside Alisz's house the night of the fire, nor his refusal to tell her the secret he insisted Mutter keep from her.

"There is no point in sulking. You might just as well face the day with a smile rather than a frown," Mutter said to Lilli one day. Lilli told Mutter she couldn't pretend to be happy when she'd never felt such misery in all her life.

"You are homesick, is all. You will become accustomed to the change. We both will. We have no choice." Lilli could tell by the sound of Mutter's voice that she did not even believe her own words.

"Then tell me what you've kept from me all these years," she said. Mutter turned away.

"I cannot tell you. You must accept that some things are not for children to know. I made a vow. I will not break my word." Lilli's cheeks were ablaze. Why was Mutter being so difficult?

Once again, she left Lilli with a hundred unanswered questions sizzling on her tongue.

# CHAPTER
# TWENTY-NINE

**T**HE SEA BREEZE SHOWERED LILLI WITH BURSTS OF SALTY air that matted her long blond hair. Standing on the weathered deck of the ship, she watched the clouds roll and rumble. That morning she had counted the marks she'd made in Alisz's book. They had been on the open sea for thirty-one days, prisoners to the constant rocking back and forth of the waves.

Secrets had been kept from her her entire life. Even Mutter refused to talk. Her life was nothing more than lies and pretence. Somehow Alisz was involved. This was no way to begin her new life with things left unresolved from her life in Württemberg.

Staring out across the water, Lilli hoped to see something, anything on the horizon. Out on the water the waves moved in gigantic gulps, gaining in strength as the day progressed. Whitecaps moved up and down, slapping the side of the ship. There was not a single solid object on the water that Lilli could see. They were but a small speck on the ocean's wide expanse, solitary and alone, yet many. There was not even another ship in sight.

The sea grew, swelling beneath gale-force winds as the day progressed. Lilli could feel the storm's mighty anger within her as she watched the clouds continue to build throughout the day. The sails were taken down. When the rain began to hammer the deck, they were herded below like cattle. Vents were closed and oil lamps snuffed out. Darkness held Lilli so tightly in its grip that she could not move. A pungent stench filled the air. Buckets were passed back and forth between those who were seasick.

Lilli's stomach heaved. A burning gush of bile rose in her throat and she forced it back down. Reaching into her bag of belongings, she took out some dried peppermint leaves to help settle her stomach. Mutter knelt nearby in prayer, clutching her Bible. Her murmurs blended with those of the other women while the ship was tossed about by the fury of the wind and waves. The sound was a haunting mixture of fear and resolve as the women begged God to keep them safe.

The children cried and wailed long into the night while the ship continued to creak and groan. Lilli feared the ship would be ripped apart at the seams. She closed her eyes and imagined that she was safe at home in her bed instead of being tossed about on the relentless, angry sea. She thought about the sweet smell inside Alisz's stillroom, and the finches warbling in the garden on summer days, and slowly, reluctantly, she fell into restless sleep. She dreamed she was back home in Württemberg, running happily through a field of lily-of-the-valley. A melodic lullaby repeated over and over, a song Lilli was familiar with.

> *The moon has been rising,*
> *the stars in golden guising*
> *adorn the heavens bright.*

*The woods stand still in shadows,*
*and from the meads and meadows*
*lift whitish mists into the night.*

*The world is stillness clouded*
*and soft in twilight shrouded,*
*so peaceful and so fair.*
*Just like a chamber waiting,*
*where you can rest abating*
*the daytime's mis'ry and despair.*

*Behold the moon—and wonder*
*why half of her stands yonder,*
*yet she is round and fair.*
*We are the ones who're fooling*
*'cause we are ridiculing*
*as our minds are unaware.*

Unable to open her eyes for even a brief moment, Lilli realized it was Alisz singing the lullaby, telling her not to worry.

By morning, the waters were calm once more. When Lilli awoke, fresh air was streaming in through the vents and the lamps were lit once again. Vater had been watching her sleep, she realized, as she opened her eyes. But before she could ask him to tell her the secret that had been kept from her, he quickly walked away. Wrapping her arms around Alisz's book for comfort, she hoped they would soon reach land. Closing her eyes, Lilli dreamed of Württemberg.

She imagined all the places she used to go to with Alisz when they searched for wild plants, and walking to the village with Mutter to buy goods at the market. She thought about the sun rising over the hills behind the home where she had lived her entire life. She dreamed of running barefoot through the meadow in the spring-time. So enthralled was she by the images playing out in her mind that she did not hear her name being called until someone gently shook her shoulder. Gasping, Lilli snapped open her eyes.

"Minna needs you." Hans was standing over her, concern written across his face. "She said you would come. There is no one else on board who can help."

"Tell her I will be there soon," said Lilli. Rummaging through her belongings, she chose one of the bags of herbs. Hurrying her way on deck to steep some tea for Minna, Lilli went over all the things Alisz had taught her about childbirth. She could only hope that she would remember it and that nothing out of the ordinary took place. This was Minna's fourth child, after all. Surely all would go well.

∾

"Are you sure this will help?" said Minna, looking up at Lilli. Her voice suggested hope, but there was fear lurking in her eyes. Minna had hoped they would reach land before the baby arrived, but that was not to be the case.

"Raspberry leaf tea is most helpful for women in childbirth," said Lilli, holding the cup to Minna's lips. Minna reached out for the tea and took a sip.

"This child is in a hurry," she said, smiling between the pains.

"They come in their own time," said Lilli, something she had heard Alisz say on several occasions. She beckoned for Minna to drink more of the tea.

"This is four times, and each time has been different," said Minna, handing the empty cup back to Lilli. "I am glad you are here." She lightly squeezed Lilli's hand. Regardless of any misgivings Lilli might have, she knew she had to keep her feelings to herself.

The dark, smelly area below deck was hardly an ideal place to bring a child into the world. But there was no other choice. She had asked Mutter to pray that all would go well. As for Lilli, she could only hope there would be no difficulties like the night Frau Ludwig's child was born. Her bag did not contain any birthing powder. She wouldn't know what to do with it anyway. There were only the raspberry leaves. They would have to do.

"He is big and strong. I can tell by the way he kicks. Hans is worried."

"He?" asked Lilli with curiosity as another pain gripped hold of Minna.

For hours Lilli remained at Minna's side, holding her hand and wiping her brow. Mutter came by several times, and each time Lilli assured her that all was well. It would just take time.

Late in the day the sharp cries of a baby echoed inside the vessel; Lilli felt nothing but relief. And as the child's first cries travelled throughout the belly of the ship, a wave of hope moved joyfully with it. Suddenly those who were downcast were now smiling, and some laughed as they looked from one to another.

"You were right," said Lilli, wrapping the baby in a blanket. "Do you have a name for him yet?"

"He will be Von," said Minna taking the child into her arms. As she gazed into his eyes, she said, "and your name means hope."

*There is a reason for everything in life*, thought Lilli, recalling Alisz's words and there is nothing more powerful than hope.

"Von," repeated Lilli thoughtfully. "I believe it is a most fitting name."

As Lilli looked down at Von lying in Minna's arms, she was reminded of the night the Ludwig baby was born. Alisz had gathered the child into her arms and introduced her to the Earth Goddess. If only she could do the same for Von. But they were at sea. The Earth Goddess was far away. As hope continued to build throughout the ship, Lilly had a thought. There *was* a goddess waiting to meet

Minna's baby. She would introduce Von to the Goddess of Hope. Gathering the baby from Minna's arms, Lilli held the child upward in her extended arms.

"Welcome to the world, little one, your home for this earthly incarnation. May hope be ever present in your heart as you journey through life. And may you recognize the blessings that have been placed before you. May your very life bring hope to all who know you."

Shortly after Von's joyous arrival, the sickness arrived. A young girl who slept not far from Mutter and Lilli was the first to come down with it. A hollow-eyed woman tended to her day and night. Holding a wet cloth to her forehead, the woman quietly whispered, "There, there...there, there," long into the night. Every now and again she dipped the cloth into a basin of briny water and returned it to the girl's forehead. Mutter watched in silence, her face pulled tight with worry.

"The herbs Alisz gave us," whispered Lilli. "Perhaps we could help."

"No, Lilli. What if we need them? There is not enough for everyone," said Mutter sharply. "We must keep our distance and hope the sickness does not find us." With so many people inside the ship, Lilli wondered if that was possible.

It did not take long for the sickness to spread among other passengers. No one was safe. Muffled sobs and low, mournful howls reached Lilli's ears at night. There was no way to escape it. She clung to Alisz's book, huddled into a small round ball as her stomach grew tight. It was impossible to eat.

"You need to keep up your strength," Mutter said, holding out some salted meat for Lilli to take. The ship was stealing Lilli's appetite, robbing her of her strength. The farther away they got from home, the sicker she became. Her clothes hung from her as the flesh began to disappear from her bones. She was so homesick for Württemberg she could hardly stand it. She longed to be on dry land, some place safe, without the constant rocking back and forth of the ship. She tried to concentrate on the outcome, the way Alisz would tell her she should. She imagined stepping off the ship and onto the shore. She pictured the trees and grassy knolls and an abundance of familiar flowers growing in the New World. She saw herself hugging Mutter and Friedrich and even Vater, so happy to have made it across the brutal Atlantic. Yet, despite all these positive thoughts, there were many times when she wondered if they would ever reach land.

The voyage dragged on with little to do. Lying in the cramped berth, Lilli would close her eyes and imagine the sunset behind the hills near her house, or that she was standing in Alisz's stillroom surrounded by dried herbs and copper kettles. Sometimes she could almost draw the sweet, savoury smells to her memory instead of the stale, stagnant air inside the ship. There were times when her imagination was the only thing that stopped her from giving into despair.

She often awoke, confused by the muffled sounds of people talking late into the night. It seemed these people never slept. She would drift back into a fitful sleep; other times she would toss and turn until morning. It was often during the quiet of Lilli's dreams that Alisz would come to her. "Tell me the secret that Mutter and Vater are keeping from me," Lilli would beg. Each time Alisz would answer, "It is a family matter, Lilli. I cannot interfere."

# CHAPTER THIRTY

THE YOUNG GIRL WAS THE FIRST TO DIE, FOLLOWED A WEEK later by the woman who had stayed by her side day and night. Surely they were mother and daughter, although Lilli did not know for sure. She had not spoken to either of them since they had boarded the ship. She had hardly spoken to anyone except Minna. The young girl had smiled at her the first day, her eyes filled with anticipation, like so many others on board. Lilli had not bothered to return the smile, nor did she say hello when the young girl spoke. Consumed in her own misery, she had not even asked their names. Now, they were both gone. Reality struck Lilli a fierce blow as she watched the body of the young girl being wrapped for burial. They might all die, each and every one of them, and Vater's dream of owning land in Nova Scotia lost with them. A dreadful lull settled over the ship as one by one the sick succumbed to their illness.

Vater said they must keep to themselves for fear that they too would be stricken.

"Speak to no one, even if they appear well. We will all make it across safely," he said, as if his words had the power to make it so. Mutter worriedly rubbed a spot on the palm of her hand. At night she whispered prayers for God to protect them.

A few days after the girl and her mother died, Mutter placed her hand upon Lilli's fevered brow and let out a soft cry. Lilli had tried to keep it a secret, hoping it was a case of seasickness and nothing more. When Mutter confirmed what she already feared, tears filled Lilli's eyes. She wanted to tell Mutter that she was sorry for falling ill but did not know how to put her fevered thoughts into words. She could only lie there looking at Mutter's agonized face. And then, as if an idea came to her like a lightning bolt, Mutter began to rummage through Lilli's belongings until she found the bag of willow bark Alisz had given her to take on the voyage.

"I will steep it. No one will have to know what it is. There is not enough for everyone," she said, hastily pulling the string on the bag. In her hurry, it fell from her hands and some of the contents scattered at her feet. In a swift movement, she snatched the bag up. Holding it to her like a sack of gold, she scooped up the loose bits of willow bark and put them back in the bag.

"But Vater," croaked Lilli. He might object to anything that involved Alisz and her herbs.

"I will not sit by and do nothing," Mutter whispered. "Nor will Vater. He understands that some plants heal. It is some of the others that he questions."

"You mean the witches' plants?" scoffed Lilli. Mutter placed a gentle hand on Lilli's head.

"You might think he is cruel, but his love for you is strong, much stronger than you realize."

Mutter returned later with the tea. She blew on it to make it ready for drinking. Vater and Friedrich stood in the background anxiously looking on.

"We are fortunate to have had Alisz as our friend," Mutter said, looking back at Vater. Lilli brought the tea to her lips and swallowed.

"Drink it all," said Vater, nodding his head with a solemn expression on his lips. "If it will help, you must drink it all."

Later, when it was Mutter and Lilli alone, Lilli looked up at Mutter. As sick as she was, she had to know the truth. "Why was Vater so frightened of my friendship with Alisz all these years?"

Mutter set down the empty cup. She sighed then looked down at Lilli.

"He was always afraid of losing you. Fear is what spurred him," she whispered, stroking Lilli's fevered cheek. "You have to know that losing a child would be unbearable. He could not bear to think of it. Alisz has a certain way about her that draws people to her. I'm sure you have seen it. It is part of her charm."

"Lose me? But that is ridiculous." Lilli turned her head away. Mutter's words did not explain a thing. As sick as she was, she could not release the stone of anger that had settled in her heart. Vater was cruel and unjust. Nothing Mutter said would change that.

"There are things you do not know about Alisz," Mutter began, choosing her words with care.

"I do not want to hear what you have to say. Alisz is our friend," said Lilli.

"This you need to know, but you must never speak of it," whispered Mutter, looking over her shoulder. "I have known Alisz my entire life, Lilli. She comes from a family of healers, women who were forced to hide what they did because those around them did not understand. I have always known what they did, how they were able to help. I was one of those who kept their secret. I did not even tell Vater...all those years I did not tell. That is how important the secret was."

"But Mutter," objected Lilli, wondering how any of this could possibly involve them now.

Mutter motioned for Lilli to listen. "For six long years, Vater and I longed for a child. Each year became more difficult for me to bear. I knew Alisz could help. I knew about the special herbs she had. So, I went to her for assistance. Only she said she would not help unless Vater was in agreement. 'Deception in any marriage will only bring problems, and I will not be an instrument of deception,' she said. So I went to Vater and told him that Alisz could help us, that we did not need to worry. But Vater refused to hear anything about Alisz or her herbs. 'There are plants that can heal, but none have the ability to conjure a child. Do you hear me, Marta? We will not bring a child into this world through the use of witchcraft. She is fooling you,' he said. I told him it was not witchcraft, that Alisz was my friend, the herbs she used were just plants that grow in the ground—plants like flax and wheat, nothing more. 'A child will come in its own time,' he said. 'We do not need that woman's help.'"

Mutter laid a hand on Lilli's forehead.

"More years passed and still nothing. My sadness deepened. Then one day I could not make myself get out of bed. Nothing Vater said or did held any interest for me. I could not eat and could barely do my work. Vater knew my sorrow. The hand of worry was upon him. I know you think he is stubborn, Lilli, but that has not always been the case. He understands more than you know. He is no different than many others in Württemberg. His beliefs have been passed down through many generations. It is not so simple for him to forget all that he has spent a lifetime fearing." Mutter dipped a cloth into some foul-smelling water and wrung it out, laying it across Lilli's forehead before continuing.

"Then the day I had waited for finally came. Vater agreed to allow Alisz to help, but he insisted that we pay her. He did not want to be in her debt. He still feared Alisz might be a witch, and he believed that to be indebted to a witch would put us in danger. He sent me with some coins and my heart sang with joy. He did this for me, Lilli. He set aside his fears for my happiness. I told him he would not be sorry. Alisz would help us have a child. It would all be worthwhile."

"Like Frau Eberhart?" whispered Lilli through fevered lips.

"Like Frau Eberhart," said Mutter, nodding. "I took Vater's message, and the coins, back to Alisz. She did not want any payment, but I told her Karl insisted. 'He is a proud man,' I told her. 'He will not take your help without giving something in return.' Finally, Alisz agreed, but it was not the payment he had expected.

"'When the child is five, bring her to me. I only ask that I get to know her and pass on the teachings. That is all the payment that is necessary.'"

"How did she know you would have a girl?"

"Alisz has her ways," said Mutter. "I'm sure you have seen this in your time with her." Lilli nodded. There was no denying Alisz's special way of knowing things.

"I begged Karl to give in to her request. 'You do not need to fear Alisz,' I told him. 'She heals the sick and delivers children safely to their mothers' arms.' He reluctantly agreed. So, I took you there when you were five, just as we had agreed upon. Vater did not like it, but he was afraid to anger Alisz. To anger a witch would put us all in danger—or so he believed. But then, the older you became the more time you spent with Alisz." Pausing, Mutter sorrowfully shook her head. "Vater has always been frightened of losing you to Alisz. He worried that she would one day take you from us. Alisz was the one responsible for your arrival, and he could not get it out of his head that she would one day want you back."

Lilli's head began to spin. She could barely make sense of what Mutter was saying. It was as if she were talking about people she did not even know.

"As I said, in the beginning we agreed for you to spend time with Alisz when you were older, but when the time finally came, Vater changed his mind. There are people who fear Alisz. They know she is different. Vater is one of those people."

"Then why did he let me go?" asked Lilli in earnest. "When the time came he could have said no. Alisz would have understood."

"I have told you, he fears Alisz. He thought something bad would happen to all of us if he went back on his word." Mutter let out another sigh. "It is my fault. I should have insisted that Alisz take the coins. It has only caused us grief. It was an agreement that should never have been made, but I wanted a child so badly—*we* wanted a child. But each time you went, each visit, Vater would fume. I should have known that one day his fear would get the better of him."

"And Friedrich?"

"Friedrich is the child who came in his own time," said Mutter, quietly nodding. "So you see we would have had a very long wait."

By now Lilli's head was throbbing, her throat dry. If only Mutter would stop talking for a moment and allow her to rest. There was so much to take in. Again Mutter felt her forehead. Reaching for Lilli's hand, she held fast.

Slipping into a fevered sleep, Lilli dreamed that she was back in Alisz's house and they were reading from her stillroom book. A soft, cool breeze entered the ship's hold and slid a soothing hand across Lilli's forehead as she slept. She could hear Mutter somewhere in the distance calling out her name, but the desire to answer her was not there.

*Do not be afraid, Lilli*, Alisz whispered in her ear. *We will see each other again in another time and another place. I promise.*

*But how will I know you?*

*When your soul sings the song of forgotten times, you will awaken to the past. But only for a short time. The memories will come and go, but our friendship will continue.*

Lilli wanted to ask Alisz what that all meant. *How odd*, she thought, *Alisz is in Württemberg and I am on a ship bound for the New World.* A peaceful feeling spiralled through her then. It was dark, with strong, warm arms that carried her away, softly, softly into another realm of consciousness where she felt nothing but peace.

☙

## NEW GERMANY, NOVA SCOTIA, 2019

"Don't be sad, Lilly," said Alice as she followed Lilly to the front door. "I know you meant well. And it was lovely to think that we were once soul-friends."

"But I was so sure. It seemed so real—Walpurgisnacht, the cinnamon-haired woman, the fires—all of it." Lilly found it hard to disguise her disappointment. She reached for the doorknob.

"Dreams can seem very real. I know how much you wanted this wonderful story to be true."

"But…" Lilly turned and looked at Alice. There was so much she wanted to say, but it wouldn't make any difference. She'd done all she could think to do, and nothing had changed. They stood in the open doorway, the full moon shining brightly overhead. Lilly looked at it with longing. Somewhere in the world they were celebrating Walpurgisnacht as the arrival of spring. Was it true that the veil between the worlds was now thinnest, or was that all a story, too?

"There's still so much we don't know or understand about the subconscious mind," said Alice, absently reaching for the ancient pendant around her neck. "This was something you needed to try, or else you'd have always wondered. But regardless, we are still friends, and we share wonderful memories in *this* lifetime. That is the important part." Seeing the stone, Lilly thought of the story Alice had told her when she was small.

"Can you tell me the story about the rainbow moonstone again?" she said. She suddenly needed to hear it. She remembered how mysterious the story had seemed when she was little.

"You remember that story?" laughed Alice, still moving the stone in her fingers. She smiled. "The story goes that the labradorite stone has been in my family for centuries." Once again, she told

Lilly of the two friends who had to say goodbye. When Alice got to the end, Lilly saw something strange happening to the labradorite stone around Alice's neck.

"Alice! The rainbow moonstone!" said Lilly as the stone began to glow brighter and brighter. Rainbow colours pulsed like a beating heart. Lilly gasped and stepped backwards as a rainbow of colours lit up the air between them. High above, the full moon beckoned them to look upward. They stood in quiet awe for a time, unable to move or even speak.

"The Night Goddess is calling to us," said Alice, looking at Lilly. Her expression had changed from surprise to that of understanding. "My dear, sweet lily-of-the-valley," she said, now smiling. There was recognition in her eyes, a song her soul remembered from long ago. "It has been a very long time."

"Alisz!" gasped Lilly, as a flood of memories washed through her. "Is it really you?"

# CHAPTER THIRTY-ONE

## ATLANTIC OCEAN, 1752

WHEN SOMEONE SHOUTED OUT, "LAND AHEAD!" LILLI felt her body stiffen. Oh, how she wanted to rush onto the deck. All those days and weeks on the ocean with not a thing in sight, to now suddenly gaze upon land again.

"I have to see," Lilli said to Mutter as she struggled to sit up. It was impossible to remain below deck knowing that somewhere trees, rocks, and mounds of earth were waiting to greet her.

"Lilli, you have come through the hardest part of your illness, but you are still not fully well."

"Please, Mutter," Lilli pleaded. "My strength is coming back. I need to see." It had been more than a week since her fever finally broke. Little by little, with each passing day, Lilli felt her health returning. Many of the other passengers had not been so lucky;

some still lay sick, while others had found their final resting place at the bottom of the sea. Each day Lilli gave a silent thank you to the Goddess for making her well.

"It is against my better judgement," Mutter finally said as she offered Lilli a steady arm to hold on to. "But you have been in the darkness of the ship for far too long. The fresh air and sunshine might do you good. And I must admit, it will be glorious to gaze upon dry land again. More than once I worried that we would not see this day come."

The wind pushed a steady stream of cool air in Lilli's face as she climbed up onto the deck. Sunlight made her squint, and she shielded her eyes until they became adjusted to the brightness of the outdoors. The fresh air brought a smile to her face for the first time in weeks. She clung to Mutter, the wind pulling on her clothes and hair. Planting her feet onto the wooden deck, she grabbed tighter to Mutter's arm. Clearly, her strength was not completely restored. It would take more time.

"Do you see it, Lilli? Do you see the land?" laughed Mutter. People were pointing and shouting.

"There is only water and waves," she said, straining to see something, anything on the horizon. And then, far off in the distance, so far she could barely make out what it was, she saw a small, raised portion of land. Her heart leaped. It was the New World. They had finally made it! She looked at Mutter. Tears where streaming down her face. Their journey was nearly over. There was a time when Lilli thought she would never feel joy in this new land. She was so tired of the sea that she did not even stop to wish that she was back in Württemberg. There was no point in dreaming of what once was. She was in the New World now. The old world she'd left behind could no longer matter. Alisz was right. It was pointless to remain with one foot rooted in the past.

Closing her eyes, Lilli breathed in the smell of the windswept sea. Her hair danced against her cheeks. It seemed an eternity since she had felt the fresh air against her skin. A few short weeks ago she would never have thought she would take pleasure in such a simple thing as this. That was before she lay in the cramped quarters below deck watching Mutter's worried face peering down at her. Each time she sipped the willow bark tea, she closed her eyes and prayed for the tea's great healing power to make her better. As she lay there in her sickness, she realized how fortunate she had been to have spent all those years learning from Alisz. It was only right that she continue to use this knowledge when she arrived in the New World. There would be people in need of her help. It was what Alisz would want.

Overhead, gulls shrieked and circled the ship, their cries filling the breeze. Lilli wished she were a bird, able to take to the sky, disappear into the blue without a care in the world, just as Friedrich had once done in her dream. As she stood on the deck watching the birds, a peaceful sensation began to eddy inside her. For the first time since they began their voyage to Nova Scotia, she did not allow her mind to wander forward or back.

"Enjoy this moment for what it is," Alisz used to say.

Alisz! It was then Lilli remembered that she had left Alisz's book unattended.

"Our belongings," she said to Mutter. "We left them below in plain sight!" She had always been careful to put her possessions in the space beneath the berth where no one could see.

"No one will harm them," said Mutter. "Everyone is too happy now and you should be, too. Our things will be fine."

Still, Lilli could not stop the uneasiness from creeping over her. She had always been so careful about Alisz's book, never allowing it out in plain sight this whole journey. Oh, why had she run off at the first mention of land, forgetting her most prized possession? She shouldn't have been so foolishly spirited away, taken in by the cries of "Land ahead!" Lilli fought to relieve the panic that was growing in her as she hurried below deck.

"Slow down," cried out Mutter. But Lilli could not slow down, could not feel at peace, until she had Alisz's book under her arm. Climbing below deck, she waited for her eyes to become accustomed to the lack of light once again. Desperation threatened to overtake her. This was taking far too long. When she could finally see enough to make her way, she stumbled toward the spot where her belongings lay. She rummaged through the bedding, through Mutter's oversized bag, where she kept everything important from the herbs Alisz had given her, to a golden lock of Friedrich's hair. Coming up empty-handed, she looked fiercely at Mutter.

"It is gone...Alisz's book is gone!"

"It must be here somewhere," said Mutter, now moving their meagre belongings about in a search of her own. Lilli knew it was useless. It simply was not there.

"It was here all along—all the while I was sick. It gave me hope, knowing that I had something that came from home. Someone has taken it!" Lilli shrieked. Tears filled her eyes.

"It has to be somewhere on this ship," Mutter said. "It could not have disappeared into thin air."

"Alisz entrusted me with her book. It was her most valued possession. I have let her down. She wanted me to have it, to take care of it, to pass down all the cures. She said it would be safe with me."

"Why is Lilli crying?" It was Friedrich, suddenly standing beside Mutter. Lilli rushed toward him and grabbed him by the shoulders.

"Do you have it?" she asked, desperate for him to tell. He had seen her with the book on several occasions, holding it tightly to her chest during her illness.

"I do not know what you are talking about," said Friedrich.

"You know very well what I mean," cried Lilli. Even in the dim light, she could see from the expression on his face that he knew more than he was saying. He had done something with the book. She was positive.

"The book Alisz gave me—where is it?" she said, digging her fingers into his shoulders.

"Leave me alone, Lilli," cried Friedrich, trying to wrench free from his sister's grip. "Alisz is a witch. She put on spell on you. Vater said the book is evil."

"Alisz is not a witch, because witches do not exist," said Lilli. Her eyes filled with anger and she drew in a tight breath. "Now, where is the book?"

Friedrich cowered as if expecting she might strike him.

"Lilli, please...you are scaring your brother," Mutter pleaded as she loosened Lilli's grip on his shoulders. Friedrich took one look at his sister and darted off like a frightened deer. Lilli did not possess the strength to run after him.

"We have to look for it," she said, not knowing where to start. There was so little light to see by, even with the lamps. The ship's hold was nearly deserted, except for those too sick to leave their berth. Most everyone else had gone above deck the moment land had been spotted. Seeing a young girl sitting close to a sick woman, Lilli hurried toward her. She froze, realizing who the girl was.

"Hilda?" All this time and Lilli had not known they were on the same ship together. "Do you remember me? I am Lilli. I was at Alisz's. She gave you some willow bark."

Hilda turned her back and hung her head down, hiding behind the straggly strands of light brown hair dangling against her shoulders. She refused to look at Lilli.

"Hilda, please. My things. Did you see anyone at my things?" Lilli asked, anxious for an answer. "My book is gone. Alisz—she gave it to me before I left Württemberg." Had Hilda seen anything? And if she had, would she even tell? Lilli had called her a spy the day she came to Alisz's cottage with the honey. What right had she to ask for Hilda's help now?

"Please," begged Lilli softly. "Alisz helped your brother get well. I am begging you. Please open your heart. Did you see someone with my book?" Desperation welled inside her chest. If she lost Alisz's book, she did not know what she would do. She dared not inhale as she waited for Hilda to speak.

The woman beside Hilda stirred, moaning as she tossed about in fevered sleep.

"You can have some of the willow bark!" said Lilli suddenly. "It is the same willow bark Alisz gave your bruder. It helped me too. I was sick and it made me well. It will work for her. It will bring the fever down." Lilli would gladly share the remedy to discover the book's whereabouts. Hilda turned toward Lilli at the mention of the willow bark, her face filled with eagerness.

"It was the boy. The one you were talking to just now. I saw him take the book. It is over there," she said pointing toward a dark corner of the ship.

"Thank you, thank you," cried Lilli, jumping up.

"This willow bark you promised...you promised to give me some," Hilda called out as Lilli hurried her way between the berths to search for the book. The lighting was dim. The glow from the lanterns did not reach into the far corners. Something on the floor caught Lilli's eye. Bending to pick it up, she saw a trail of tattered paper in front of her. Falling to her knees, she grabbed the bits of parchment and held them up toward the light.

She could not cry. Her tears simply would not let go.

# CHAPTER
# THIRTY-TWO

**T**INY BITS OF WILLOW BARK SWIRLED ABOUT AS THE WATER churned and bubbled. Lilli stared down into the tea, mesmerized. She couldn't imagine what had possessed Friedrich to destroy Alisz's book. It was all she had of Alisz.

"It is fear," said Mutter in a quiet voice, steam rising from the pot as the willow bark swirled about in the boiling water. "Friedrich does not understand how much the book means to you." She paused before adding, "And he wants to please Vater. More than anything, he wants to please Vater."

"I shall never speak to him again," Lilli said spitefully. Her heart was tight with anger. She did not expect the knot to loosen. Mutter sighed as she handed Lilli a cup of the steeped tea.

"He is your brother, Lilli; of course you will speak to him. You must not allow anger to rule your heart. You will forgive when the time is right."

When the tea had cooled sufficiently, Lilli tipped the cup up to the woman's lips.

"This will help," she told Hilda. Clutching the cup with shaky hands, the woman slowly sipped the tea while Hilda looked on with apprehension.

"Vater and Jakob are already dead," said Hilda turning back toward Lilli. "I do not know what I will do if Mutter does not get better. There is no one else. If only there was something I could do," she said, her lips quivering as she spoke. "I have prayed, but it has not helped."

Lilli's heart went out to the girl. Although she was still angry with Vater and Friedrich, she could not imagine what it would be like to arrive in the New World all alone. How wrong she had been about Hilda the first day she came knocking at the stillroom door, and how certain she had been that Hilda was the one who would betray Alisz. Little did she know at the time that *she* would be the one responsible for putting Alisz's life in jeopardy.

"The willow bark will bring down the fever," Lilli reassured her. "But for now you must think positive thoughts. You must imagine her happy and well. See it in your mind's eye as if it has already happened. Our thoughts are more powerful than you can imagine."

"My mind's eye? What is that?"

"Your imagination—that part of you that allows dreams to enter."

"Vater's dream was for us to live in Nova Scotia," said Hilda.

"Then you must honour his dream by doing just that. Now, think only positive thoughts."

"I will," said Hilda as a reluctant smile crossed her face.

Lilli began gathering up the torn bits of paper and putting them in her bag. "I heard what you said to the girl," said Mutter, now helping Lilli collect the remnants of Alisz's book. "Alisz would be proud of you."

"Proud? Of me? The foolish one who could not keep her book safe from harm?" Lilli shook her head as she spoke. She had failed to protect the one thing Alisz had entrusted her with. There was nothing to be proud of. She was Alisz's soul-friend and she had let her down.

Mutter spoke firmly when she said, "Yes, proud. You gave that girl something she desperately needed—hope. That is the greatest gift there is. When hope is gone, we are left with nothing. Alisz taught you that."

"But—"

"No, Lilli, the book is gone. There is nothing that will bring it back. No amount of grief or anger or sorrow on your part. You must move on. You will recover from this loss, I promise. And what's more, you will find something good in what now seems like a tragedy. In time you will discover this hope for yourself. You did not spend all those years in Alisz's company for nothing. Alisz is a wise woman, and she has passed that same wisdom on to you. Perhaps, over time, when you remember the cures, you will write them down in a book of your own, just as the women in Alisz's family did."

"I could not possibly make my own book," said Lilli, shaking her head. Did Mutter not realize what she was saying?

"Everything must have a beginning, and all beginnings start with someone. You can be that someone."

Tears filled Lilli's eyes as she considered Mutter's words. "But what if I do not want a new beginning?"

"It is not always what we want to do, but what we are called to do. When the time comes, you will find the courage you need."

As much as she resisted the idea, Lilli knew Mutter was right. Alisz would not want her to wallow in self-pity. The book was gone, nothing would change that, but if she gathered up the torn pieces and placed them together she might be able to write some of it down. She had spent time memorizing some of the cures during the voyage; surely that information had stayed with her. Lilli finally picked up the leather-bound cover and held it to her chest.

"There is so much to be remembered," she said, feeling suddenly overwhelmed by the idea. Reproducing the book would be a great undertaking.

"Time, dear Lilli. Time," said Mutter, laying a gentle hand on her shoulder.

Lilli drew in a cleansing breath. Alisz often said that all things heal with time. Mutter was right, she might remember a great deal once she began writing things down. And these people who already live the in New World, the ones Alisz spoke of, perhaps she was right, too; perhaps they would share their wisdom with her. If all went well, over time, she would have a book of her own, one that Alisz would be proud of. Taking another deep breath, Lilli raised her head, determined to think the same positive thoughts she had encouraged Hilda to do. She would honour her friendship with Alisz by remembering all the things she had taught her over the years.

"Are you still angry with me?"

Lilli looked up into Friedrich's small, round face.

"I am sorry that I made you sad. I thought the book was evil, that it had made you sick...because it belonged to Alisz. Vater said she is a witch."

"Vater is mistaken. Alisz is not a witch, Friedrich. She has knowledge. She knows how to make people well. There is nothing evil in that. To make others well—it is a gift."

"But Vater said..."

Lilli closed her eyes, asking the Goddess for patience and understanding. Friedrich was a nine-year-old boy. There was much he did not understand. His heart truly was ruled by fear, but she could change that by giving him knowledge.

"Vater does not understand these things...but maybe one day he will. You both saw how the willow bark tea made me well." Friedrich nodded. "It was not magic. Just bark from a tree boiled in water. The willow tree has healing properties, properties that come from nature, and all plants come from God. These are the things Alisz knows about. It is how she helps people. She does not use magic or witchcraft."

"Then you are no longer angry with me?" asked Friedrich, now helping to pick up the tattered bits of paper.

Lilli looked at Friedrich and smiled softly. "How could I stay angry with you?" she said, tousling his hair.

"Will you make another book?"

Lilli stopped gathering the pieces and smiled. "It may take many years to write down all the cures," she said to Friedrich. "But one day I will start a book when we get settled in our new home."

Later, with the cool, salty air stroking her face, Lilli watched the land come closer into view. She looked around at the people standing on deck and saw Minna holding Von in her arms. She smiled. For the first time since she'd begun this journey to the New World, Lilli truly felt the hope that Mutter spoke about. While she could not get back the things that had been lost, she could face tomorrow with determination to make the most of what life had to offer.

"I shall miss you, Alisz," she whispered to the breeze, "but I shall remember."

As the cool breeze danced across the deck of the ship, Lilli was sure she could hear Alisz's voice in the wind.

*Do not be sad, dear Lilli. We will meet again one day in another place and another time.*

## NEW GERMANY, NOVA SCOTIA, 2019

"The water is perfect. Stop stalling and come in. You said you were ready." Lilly waited at the water's edge for Alice to join her. A light breeze was blowing across the lake. The sun produced small jewels on the water as tiny waves skipped up and down. In the sky, a hawk screeched down at them.

"Give me time," said Alice. Closing her eyes, she stood on the shore, taking some deep breaths.

"Remember what you learned in your meditation class. Don't let your fears rule you," said Lilly, stepping into the water.

"I'm doing that now. I'm trying to centre my mind and relax. But you won't be quiet."

"The water's not going to bite," said Lilly, wading into the lake.

"I'm not so sure."

"Try getting comfortable just being in the water. You don't have to worry about pool lessons yet."

"Oh, joy...pool lessons. Terrifying, yet a necessary evil if I want to conquer this. I can hardly wait." Alice stepped closer to the water's edge, her eyes still closed, until she could feel the cool wetness lapping at her toes. While she sounded less than enthusiastic, it had been her idea to finally face her fear of water, a fear she had wanted to overcome all her life. Lilly had promised to help.

As her foot reached further into the water, Alice looked at Lilly and smiled. "Do you suppose I drowned in another lifetime?"

"You always say that," said Lilly. Alice inched her way into the water, stopping every now and then to take a cleansing breath.

"You know, they *do* say our deepest fear comes from something that happened in a past life."

"I should do some research on that," said Lilly, thinking once again about what had happened on Walpurgisnacht, how at the exact moment when the veil between the worlds became thinnest, she remembered a garden, and a room with plants hung up to dry, and even a leather-bound book. As Alice's moonstone pendant glowed a rainbow of colours, it was as if the past and the present had become one. She recognized Alice as her soul-friend from another time. And now, weeks later, although many of those memories had faded, the knowledge that they were soul-friends still existed. They would always have that connection even as they created new memories in this lifetime. Perhaps next year on Walpurgisnacht, with the help of the rainbow moonstone, they would be able to catch a glimpse of those memories again.

As they walked home that afternoon, a warm breeze on their backs, Lilly stopped suddenly when she saw the cornflowers blooming in Alice's garden. "They weren't blooming earlier today," she said with surprise.

"They must have opened while we were at the lake. They're my favourite, you know," said Alice.

"You mean, along with almost every other flower in the world?" laughed Lilly.

"Did I ever tell you the story of how the Queen of Prussia hid her children in a field full of cornflowers to save them from Napoleon's army?" said Alice.

"How do you know all these things?" Alice was forever telling little stories and superstitions around plants. Lilly loved hearing them.

Alice smiled. "To keep the little ones quiet, she made them wreaths by weaving the cornflowers together."

"It must have been frightening," said Lilly, picturing it in her mind.

"Oh, but that's not all. When one of her children later became Emperor, he made the cornflower the national flower of Germany to honour his mother." Alice smiled. "So, you see, everything happens for a reason."

Moving toward the brilliant blue flowers, Alice closed her eyes and said, "Dear cornflower, may I pick one of your beautiful blooms for Lilly?" Pausing briefly, she plucked a flower from the stem.

"A gift from across time," she said, handing it to Lilly. And as Lilly reached out to take the flower from her soul-friend, the rainbow moonstone around Alice's neck made a quick pulse. Lilly's eyes grew wide with delight. Possibly, quite possibly, when Walpurgisnacht came around again, the rainbow moonstone would once again allow them a small glimpse into the past. Lilly smiled as she breathed in the cornflower's light, sweet scent. She could hardly wait.

ANGELA HAGGERTY

**L**AURA BEST HAS HAD OVER FORTY SHORT stories published in literary magazines and anthologies. Her first young adult novel, *Bitter, Sweet*, was shortlisted for the Geoffrey Bilson Award for Historical Fiction for Young People. Her middle grade novel *Flying with a Broken Wing* was named one of Bank Street College of Education's Best Books of 2015, and its follow-up, *Cammie Takes Flight*, was nominated for the 2018 Silver Birch Award. Her most recent middle grade book, a prequel to the Cammie series, *The Family Way*, was released in Spring 2021. Her first novel for adults, *Good Mothers Don't*, was published in 2020 and shortlisted for the Dartmouth Book Award for Fiction. She lives in East Dalhousie, Nova Scotia, with her husband, Brian. Visit lauraabest.wordpress.com.